BEAR

DOWN

✿

BEAR

NORTH

FLANNERY
O'CONNOR
AWARD
FOR
SHORT
FICTION

Nancy Zafris,
Series Editor

Melinda
Moustakis

BEAR

DOWN

❀

BEAR

NORTH

Alaska Stories

The University of Georgia Press
Athens and London

Paperback edition published in 2012 by
The University of Georgia Press
Athens, Georgia 30602
www.ugapress.org
© 2011 by Melinda Moustakis
Designed by Mindy Basinger Hill
Set in 12 /15 pt Vendetta Medium

Printed digitally in the United States of America

The Library of Congress has cataloged the hardcover
edition of this book as follows:

Moustakis, Melinda, 1982 –
Bear down, bear north : Alaska stories / by Melinda Moustakis.
x, 158 p. ; 23 cm. — (The Flannery O'Connor Award for Short Fiction)
ISBN-13: 978-0-8203-3893-4 (hardcover : alk. paper)
ISBN-10: 0-8203-3893-1 (hardcover : alk. paper)
1. Wilderness areas—Alaska—Fiction.
2. Frontier and pioneer life—Alaska—Fiction.
3. Families—Fiction. 4. Survival—Fiction. 5. Short stories.
6. Alaska—Fiction. I. Title.
PS3613.O88B43 2011
813'.6—dc22   2011010451

Paperback ISBN-13: 978-0-8203-4490-4
ISBN-10: 0-8203-4490-7

British Library Cataloging-in-Publication Data available

For my mother and father,

Constance and Michael, for their

love and support and guidance.

For Sonny, my uncle who takes

me fishing and tells me stories.

For Mike, Melaina,

Sam, and Kamal.

CONTENTS

ACKNOWLEDGMENTS

I would like to thank all the literary journals that published previous versions of the following stories: "Trigger" was originally published as "MooseBlind" *in Kenyon Review Online* 3, no. 3 (Summer 2010); "The Mannequin in Soldotna" appeared in *Conjunctions 54: Shadow Selves*; "The Weight of You" in *Cimarron Review*, no. 166 (Winter 2009); "Us Kids" in *Alaska Quarterly Review* 26, nos. 1 and 2 (Spring and Summer 2009); "This One Isn't Going to Be Afraid" in *The Massachusetts Review* (Winter 2009); "Point MacKenzie" in *The Tusculum Review* 6 (2010); "Miners and Trappers" in *Kenyon Review* 33, no. 4 (Fall 2011); "Bite" in *Storyglossia*, no. 39; "Some Other Animal" in *American Short Fiction*; "Mr. Fur Face Needs a Girlfriend" in *Alaska Quarterly Review* 29, nos. 1 and 2 (Spring and Summer 2011); "They Find the Drowned" in *Hobart* (no. 12); "What You Can Endure" in *New England Review* 32, no. 1; "The Last Great Alaskan Lumberjack Show" in *Beloit Fiction Journal* 24 (Spring 2011).

I would like to thank my parents for their support and senses of humor and for everything they have done for me over the years. And my Uncle Sonny for his generosity and his big bear of a heart, for sharing his stories and fishing expertise and for allowing me to summer on the river. An immense thank you to Nancy Zafris and University of Georgia Press for giving this book a chance.

I would like to thank all of my teachers over the years, but especially Jaimy Gordon, Stuart Dybek, Kellie Wells, and my literature professors at Western Michigan University; Pam Houston, Lucy Corin, and Lynn Freed, who I worked with while at UC Davis; Susann Cokal, Kevin

Clark, Paula Huston, John Hampsey, and Larry Inchausti at Cal Poly San Luis Obispo; and Mr. Seward and Mr. Pipkin.

I would like to thank The WMU Crowd: especially Beth Marzoni, who spent hours helping me revise this book; Rachel Swearingen, who helped me survive the last four years; Emily Stinson, who came to Kalamazoo just in time; Adeena Reitberger; Jessi Phillips; Cindy St. John; Maggie Andersen; Mark Turcotte; Kathy Zlabek, who came up with the title of this book; Hilary Selznick; Kory Shrum; Meghann Meeusen; Kate Dernocoeur; Adam and Kim Clay; James Miranda and Lauren Goldberg; R.A. Riekki, Michele Coash, Michael Fischer; Soup Night; the Tuesday Pilsen Club; and the Thursday Poker Night Players.

The Graduate College at WMU for awarding me a Graduate Student Research Grant.

Novelist John Lescroart and the UC Davis English Department for the Maurice Prize in Fiction contest, which this book won in 2010.

The Davis Crew: especially the wonderful readers of the Fiction Class of 2006.

The River Crew: especially John aka "Mots" and Carol Motsinger, Marnie and Greg Olcott and the Fam, Dan and Sean and Sam Mc-Dowell, Brad Snodgrass, Rachel and Benji Smith, Frank's drift boat and all the Reuters, Tasha and Brooks Queen, Joe from Hell, Dean Vogt, Todd Arndt, Frank Komarek, Todd Larson, and Pam Butcher, who helped make a beautiful book out of my work before it was ever published.

Friends I've known for many years: Leah and Jared Davis, Kate Asche and Charlie McComish, Nikki Hootman, and Jennifer Ortega-Briggs.

Also, a thank you to my Uncle James and Aunt Kitty (not to be confused with Kitty in the book), who take me fishing for halibut and ling cod.

"Oh, to grace how great a debtor..."

BEAR

DOWN

✻

BEAR

NORTH

TRIGGER

You were conceived on a hunting stand, they say.

Which means: We had no other place.

The homestead is full of my mother's siblings. On the stove, a pot of potato chow big enough to feed twenty. See my mother, back roughed against the wooden platform in the trees. See my father, finger on the trigger—in case.

You have to gut a moose right away, they say, or the meat rots in its skin.

Which means: We couldn't keep our hands off each other.

The night of my making, my father shot a moose through the eye, through the skull and brain and bone, through to the other side. My mother found the red-tipped bullet in the summered dirt. They keep it on the mantle next to a sepia photo—them steering the rack of the dead bull.

They say, you came into the world with a bang.

Which means: Do something to deserve us.

THE MANNEQUIN
IN SOLDOTNA

THE MANNEQUIN

She stands in the lobby of the hospital, naked. Lures and spinners and spoons and flesh flies and fish hooks cover her body. There are metallic wings and blades, mirrored and speckled jangles, feathers, fur, hair, painted beads in bright gloried purples and reds and yellows all to catch a rainbow, a dolly, a red, a king in the Kenai River.

Someone comes in with a hook in a nose or lip or neck or hand. The doctor shakes her head. The hook digs deep and pulls, the barb snagging muscle, and she pushes it through. The patient sighs with relief as the bloodied hook clangs in the metal tray. Blood seeps through cotton and the doctor replaces the gauze. Sometimes there are stitches. Today only tape.

After the patient leaves, the doctor holds the hook under the tap. She dips it in disinfectant. On the way, she passes the nurses' station and says, "I've got another one."

The nurses follow in their white, padded shoes.

"Guess," she says.

The nurses point to spots of open flesh on the mannequin. There. No, there.

The doctor touches the arch of the mannequin's foot. "Here," she says.

There are few spots left.

"Will they ever learn?" she says.

RIVER AND ISLAND

What is the sound of a river? The sound of line breaking the surface? The Kenai is a thick vein of brown and runoff from the thaw flows from the mountains, from Wally's Creek and the lower Killey, and wraps around the island where the doctor has a cabin. The Kenai is a rope, choking off a piece of land with a slow, snaking hold.

RUN

The salmon swim from river into ocean. They fatten up on shrimp and squid, growing until they are two of themselves. Thousands of miles after, the salmon ache for the milky blue waters of the Kenai. Their bodies quiver, and with one sudden pulse of blood, they turn degrees of north, they turn toward home.

HOOK

Two buddies go for rainbows at The Kitchen, where Skilak Lake meets the Kenai River. The morning is early and condensation covers the boat, the tackle box, the seats. They haven't been fishing in a while because one had a bad fall, a bad break in the leg. There's a metal pin in the bone. They drink coffee with Jack-Slack.

The one with the bad leg hooks a bow. The other reels in and secures his hook so he can net.

The bow is a fighter. He flips and jumps and makes a scene. The one strains and puts most of his weight on his good leg. "He's right there," says the one.

But the other misses with the net.

"You going blind?" says the one.

"At least I have two good legs," says the other.

"Just bag him this time."

The other stands poised, net in hand. The bow twists under the water and spits the hook. The line jerks free. The one wobbles and puts a hand on the seat to steady himself. He throws down his rod.

"I'll get the next one," says the other.

The one huffs and punches a fist into the seat. "Sure," he says. He bends down to pick up the rod, but he bends wrong. He slips a little on the deck and falls, his head hitting the other rod sitting in the holder. The other helps him up. There's blood and he's attached to the rod—the top of his ear has caught the hook.

"Pierced straight through," say the other. He cuts the line and goes to cut the barb off the hook.

"Leave it," says the one. "I want a story about me catching a bow with a hook in my ear."

The mannequin is mapped with flesh flies, rabbit fur, and yarn and thread. The doctor jabs the hook into the left side of the head where an ear would be. The man had the hook in the right ear, but that side is full.

RIVER AND ISLAND

What is the sound of a river? Glaciers melting? The echo of air and light? The Kenai is a dull shade of dust. The edges of stillwater clear— the edges reflect small winks of sun. No one knows where the river ends and the island begins.

RUN

The stars, the sun, and the moon make coordinates of refracted light. These and the smell of gravel guide them to the Kenai's mouth. Their skin glimmers like knives and their meat turns red. After a heavy rain, the water rises and they charge the river. They grow hooked snouts and wolves' teeth.

TWO PATCHES

A man and his son are in a bad way. They drift down the Kenai on a raft. Neither wishes to talk. The man brought his son hoping they could find the words. They find neither words nor fish. There are two patches on the raft—dark blue rubber cut into squares. The glue surrounding the squares makes a glossy splotch against the faded sides.

The man steers around a gravel spit. His son prepares to reel in, but the line bobs. He sets the hook and the line pays out. "I got one," he says. And the bow is a beauty—a twenty-two-inch female with a rounded head and nickel-silver shine. The son releases her.

"We're allowed one for dinner," says the man.

"Too pretty," says his son. He aims the line to cast. The man walks behind him to put up the net. The hook sails through the air and the man feels a sharp pain in his eye. He covers the eye with his hand.

"Don't touch it," says the son.

The hook prevents the man's eyes from closing when he blinks, and when he blinks the pain spikes. His thumb and forefinger pry his eyelid open.

"Drive," says the man.

The son beaches the raft on the bank. He runs up to the cabin door and knocks, looks in the window. Empty. But the next cabin has an answer.

The man stands on the bank. Liquid blurs his vision and there's a slicing pain, but the pain feels good.

The doctor removes the hook from the eye. She doesn't flinch. But standing in front of the mannequin this time, she pauses at the colorful geography—spin 'n' glows, watermelons, wooly buggers. "I'm sorry," she says, and she stabs the mannequin's eye.

RIVER AND ISLAND

What is the sound of a river? Edges dissolving? Vanishing stones? The Kenai is a shade of dust. Underneath the skirts of the island, the river's tides pull through, sweeping, branches and sticks and muck swirl in the boils. Webs of decomposed humpy flesh float down in delicate globs.

RUN

They fight the river, the rocks, bears, hook and line. The salmon do not eat and their stomachs close. Their skin deepens with red, and green hoods their heads.

CLEAN

Two brothers stand on the old dock. One shows the other how to filet the salmon so that they don't lose meat. The knife is new.

The older steps back and hands the knife to the younger. The younger has the knife perched over the salmon. A rotted plank breaks beneath them.

The younger falls first and the knife gashes the forearm of the older. They stand on the rocks and the splintered wood surrounds their waists. Blood from the gash drips onto the dock.

The father drives them to the hospital for stitches.

The doctor says, "Lucky. A clean cut. No veins or tendons."

The older doesn't blame the younger. The younger blames the wood, the rotting, the dock—but not the knife.

The doctor passes by the mannequin—there weren't any hookings that day. And if there were, where would she put the hook? She is running out of space and soon she'll have to start a new mannequin.

RIVER AND ISLAND

The island's reflection is stretched over the river's surface, wavering on water. Are you coming or going, river? The Kenai, milk tinged with ribbons of green and brown, is raging, is at rest.

RUN

And the river is loaded—a frenzy of salmon full of eggs and milt and muscle. Coming or going?

LIP

One night a guide heads to the bar after a day on the river and meets a girl. She's a waitress at Suzie's, saving up for college and a ticket out of Alaska. She's been given a scholarship for jumping hurdles. He just got out of the navy, was stationed in Texas, but he says Hawaii. She's always wanted to go to Hawaii. He picks her up at Bing's Landing on a Wednesday, so he can tell her more about the islands and the clear, dazzling water he's only seen in magazines.

She brings food from the diner, chicken and fries and biscuits. He brings an appetite.

They catch two dollies. He keeps one.

"I thought we were letting them go," she says.

"Allowed one a day," he says.

The sun burns the top of her shoulders. He wonders if she'll peel, have lighter patches underneath. They stop to eat at a secluded bank.

"Smile," he says.

She clenches her jaw, but her mouth quivers.

"You can smile, can't you?"

To spite her—her lips obey.

He smiles back. "Hawaii is beautiful," he says. "You should come with me."

"What island do you live on?" she asks.

He moves closer, circles a fingertip on her pink shoulder. "Does this hurt?"

She shrugs him off. "Let's catch some more fish."

He grabs her arm. "Let's stay here."

She could run. Scream. Pick up a rock. An old hook on the ground. She smiles at him again and sits down, places her left hand over the hook. She kisses his mouth and readies the weapon in her left hand. She traces his lips with her fingertip, reaches inside toward his teeth and exposes the red-jeweled flesh of his bottom lip. She stares straight into his eyes. Then she shoves the hook down through, piercing him. He crumples with the pain and she leaves him on the bank and drives away. He'll have a scar and never forget. She'll never leave home without a hook in her pocket.

The boy arrives alone. His story is vague. His friend hooked him while casting. The doctor notices how his eyes dart up and down her body— she isn't as gentle as she should be when removing the hook from his lip. The point of entry is intimate and the hook is old—it uncovers his lie.

"An accident?" she says.

"I told you," he says.

"Tell your friend to buy some new hooks," she says.

The doctor smiles as she traces the exact spot with her finger and jams the hook into the mannequin's flesh, in the space below lip, above chin.

RIVER AND ISLAND

What is the sound of a river? Babble? Chatter? The Kenai is a green of silt, jade and pearl and debris. The island is sinking, caving in.

RUN

They hurdle rapids and boulders, day after day. They turn a bend and the currents slow. This. Here. Their first tang of river. The gravel where they were born. The female shudders, flexes her back, and the eggs drop, loose and translucent. The male follows and fertilizes the redd.

BACK

Two buddies backtroll for kings. They've anchored the boat and they're tossing back a few beers, waiting for the big one to hit.

"You seen a green tiger-striped glow?" says Jay. "Thought I'd try it next reel-in."

"You look in the box?" says D.

"Can't see how it couldn't be here," says Jay.

"Should be in that twenty you got rigged up." D fidgets with the reel. "Packed drift. Don't know how no one's hooking in."

"Just wait until I find this glow," says Jay.

D settles down into his seat. "Might as well catch what I can—get a little shut-eye."

"You do that," says Jay.

D gets into the groove of sleep, makes a racket with his pawpaw snore.

"Useless," says Jay.

D's line smacks with a bite.

"You've got a live one," says Jay.

D jumps to attention and sets the hook. Jay reels in his line and primes the net.

"That's my green glow," says Jay.

"My yellow one," says D.

"You sure?"

"Just looks green underwater."

Jay bags the king. He holds the mallet over the head. Stops. "That is my glow."

"No, it's mine," says D.

The king flops on the deck between them.

"You telling me you got the same exact one? The one I was missing?"

"Give me the mallet," says D. "Then we'll fix this."

"You're a liar," says Jay. "I got it made special at Townie's. Custom Mylar wings." He moves toward the flailing king. "You don't deserve this fish."

"Don't you dare," says D.

Jay bends down and throws the king overboard. D flies at him in a fury. The two wrestle down to the deck floor. D howls a kicked-dog howl and Jay releases his grip.

"You all right?"

D turns on his side. He's got the tackle, the hook jammed right in the meat of his back.

Jay touches the hook.

D whimpers.

And because D's made that sound and Jay thinks he deserves it, he touches the hook again and waits for D to wince. "Don't move," says Jay. "Don't do nothing."

Jay asks the doctor if he can keep the green spin'n'glow.

"The big fish here has to decide," says the doctor, pointing at D.

"I don't want it," says D. "And I don't want him to have it neither."

"Fair enough," she says.

"Put it on that voodoo thing in the lobby," says D.

The doctor feels, then, each puncture, each hook, prick her body, a wave starting from her head and cresting down to her feet. And every hook is attached to a line, a fishing rod, and a body holding the rod, and each body is covered in hooks that tear open flaps of flesh, small pockets of bleeding, a web.

Two days later, the doctor walks past the mannequin with three charts in her hand and her eye corners Jay running out of the lobby.

"Stop him," she yells and she charges after him.

A man in a flannel jacket grabs Jay, tackling him to the pavement. The doctor holds out her hand.

"Give it to me," she says.

"No," says Jay.

The man in the flannel jacket pries the green spin'n'glow from Jay's fingers.

She's standing over him and shaking her head. "You don't know what you've done," she says.

RIVER AND ISLAND

The Kenai is a vein of turquoise, clear and glass and settled. The river cradles the island in its arms, lullabies the trees. It's not day or night or morning and the doctor is still awake, sitting near an unlit campfire, and across the river a fisherman throws his line—cast, drift and follow, cast.

RUN

The days are long and thin. The salmon keep to the shallows near rotting trees. With reaching fingers, the Kenai tugs at their tails, drawing them to the channel. The salmon wrestle the water, tap their last beats of blood, and when the river wins, they drift and fodder downstream. Their bodies are carried, broken, and fed to the currents.

THE NEW MANNEQUIN

A man boats across Skilak Lake at the head of the Kenai. Three boys throw rocks from the shore. When he is close, he sees their target—a log in the water. But it isn't a log. He tells the boys to get on out of there, to go home. But all they do is walk away and look on from a distance. He's heard a woman has been missing for a week. A drowned body sinks and bloats up and eventually floats back to the top. She's wearing a green jacket so he grabs the collar with his right hand and drives with his left. Her hair covers her face. He drives to shore and tells the boys to look away but they stare. He's in a couple feet of water so he cuts the engine and jumps out, holds her and the boat and walks them both to land. The boys come and take the boat. He has no choice so he drags her to shore. Because she is out of the water, because she has been missing for a week, her face falls off, and there is a crater in the skull, a bullet wound. He turns his back. The boys have covered their eyes. He struggles with the latch on the box seat. The gulls announce themselves as they fly over, descending in a flock, and he hurries to unfold the tarp and cover her. The wind picks up the tarp and uncovers her face without a face. He gathers rocks to weight down the corners. The boys throw rocks at the gulls.

The mannequin is full—clothed in deer hair, elk, rabbit, quail feathers, wire, hooks, a dress of many colors. And next to her is a new mannequin, a blank landscape. The doctor has heard the news about the girl they found in the river, the bullet wound in the back of the head. The girl's name is Casey Bakten—she lived with her mother in Sterling, the town next to Soldotna. The doctor looks at the new mannequin, but there's nothing she can do to record this—it's too big. And the doctor has to sit down a while because she's thinking that somewhere in the world there's another one happening as she sits there next to a clumsy table of magazines. She jams a fist into her stomach, and she's there, standing in the river and her waders fill up with water, weigh down in the current, and then she snags the bottom and she steps back toward the bank, slips, and then she is sliding under, gone, and the current takes her, drags her by the ankles into the swarm. She is melting, liquid and heat, and her limbs fuse to her body, first her feet, her arms, her fingers. She streams metallic, a core of red cooling into the shape of a bullet.

"Only hooks," she says to the new, blank mannequin. "I've got one fight in me."

RIVER AND ISLAND

The doctor sits on the bank. The sun slips from the ledge and dissolves into the mountains. She's thinking of bodies, small hooks of metal,

the first tang of river. The first tang and sound—small whisperings
at the halo of her neck.

RUN

The doctor knows the new mannequin is waiting for her. But how to
mark the mannequin for this story? A man has a comfortable cabin
on the Kenai and he lives alone. His days on the river are either too
slow or too fast. On the too fast days he stops his truck at Good Time
Charlie's and picks up a girl, her hair parted on the side. The first thing
he marks—the white line of scalp. He feels good and he feels rich so
he offers her double and he drives her to his cabin. They spend an
hour or so together and the girl's laughter fills up his cabin where he
lives alone. He cooks a meal. Then he takes the girl on a ride in his
small plane—he'd gotten his pilot license so he could scout moose
and bears. The girl likes the view of the river and mountains and sips
wine from the bottle he's brought along. He lands in a bowled spot
somewhere and offers her more money to strip. She makes a show,
throws her green jacket at him sitting in the pilot's seat. He smiles
as she tosses away her clothes, smiles as she tries not to shiver. She
stands before him, naked, and he says, "Take off your jewelry." She
undoes her bracelet clasp, slides off her rings, and pulls the hoops out
of her ears. He's still smiling, but she doesn't know what else to do. He
takes out a rifle and fires, shooting to her left. "What are you doing?"
she yells. He fires again. "Run," he says. She turns and runs. She can
see shade up the hillside and she pumps her arms. He shoots close to
hear her scream. And then he shoots her in the back. She crawls and
aims for the trees. When he walks up to her, she moans. To him, it is
the same sound that the bears make.

THE WEIGHT

OF YOU

Your fishing pole slams and you jump up and yank the rod out of the holder.

"Easy," Jack says. "Wait for him to take it." Another tug and he's yelling, "Set that sonofabitch," as you pull up to set the hook and reel in and pull up again—a double set.

"Fish On. Fish On," you shout.

"She's got a Fish On," he calls out to the rest of the river. He holds up the net, the signal for "We've got a king on our line—get the hell out of the way." A few boats give you space, but the guide boats full of tourists stay where they are. The king starts running upriver and Jack pulls anchor and rows away from the tip of Eagle Rock. You hang on as the king rips out line and you crank the reel to bring in the slack. The pole tip noodles into the river and when you clench your jaw and lean into the fight, the king spits the hook.

You've lost the takedown and Jack says, "You're supposed to be the lucky one, Gracie," and you know what your brother always says next, "God helps you and he fucks with me."

You're anchored up again and he splashes V8 into an empty plastic water bottle, and then fills it up with vodka. "You want a Holy Mary?" he says with a smile, knowing you'll say no because it's eight in the morning and he's the only one who likes them Holy instead of Bloody.

"I've got coffee," you say and raise the thermos.

"It better be spiked," he says.

"Your Island Special," you say, which means whiskey and cream. Three hours on the Kenai backtrolling for kings, and you still haven't upped and told him what you wanted to say.

He is five years older than you, married with three kids. One of the reasons you're out fishing is your sister-in-law, Jean. She wants you to talk to him about his drinking and calls you two, three times a day at Fred Meyer where you work as a grocery clerk. He's always been extreme, but she says he's just taken out a second life insurance policy.

"Who needs two?" she said. "He keeps telling me he's going to die young. He just knows it."

For a couple of years growing up, he was obsessed with the afterlife. When things got bad, he had you help him make a list of ways you could get there faster: drowning in a river or bathtub, bullet wound, drinking lighter fluid, axe to the neck, holding your breath, jumping into a fire. He tried once—climbed as high as he could up a spruce tree in your yard and jumped. But it was winter and Anchorage was having record snowfall and he gave himself a good headsmack, sloshed his brain is what your mother said after he started throwing up, but she didn't take him to the doctor.

A cloud sweeps over and he stands up and raises his bulky arms to the sky. "Jesus, give us some sun, goddamnit. I only get a couple days a year." The Matthew brothers, who he calls Doormat and Hazmat, laugh in their boat and say, "You tell 'em, Jack." The tourists stare at your brother—you can tell who they are because, as Jack says, they're "shit on oars" and are wearing matching blue jackets and have already bumped into your drift boat. Peppered beard at thirty-one, biceps the size of your head, and now waving his flannel shirt and telling the clouds to move—Jack is what they'd call Alaskan bush. Tourists come to see moose and eagles and to catch kings they've only dreamed about. Your brother is a bonus.

"I've got to take a piss," he says and grabs the PVC pipe and steps past you. He faces front with the tourists, unzips his pants, holds the pipe in place. You hear the tourist-woman gasp. "This is how you do it on the Kenai," he says. "Dick in a stick."

He starts on another Holy Mary.

"Maybe you shouldn't," you say.

"Not you, too," he says. "I've given up all of my crazy shit. This is all I got left. This and Drift Mondays. You hear this, Hazmat? G-string here wants me to quit drinking."

"Shit," says Hazmat.

"Shit is right," Jack says.

You're the little sister and he's the big brother, but the word "big" doesn't even come close to what he is. He was your kidding wink and punch in the arm, your prince of cards, your freckled mirror. You shared a room at the house in Trapper Creek. Foil over the windows to keep out the summer sun. A ball of foil, wide as a dinner plate, hanging from the ceiling, and when the bruising sounds from the living room got too loud, he'd shine a flashlight on it and say, "Tell me about the moon, Gracie," and the moon was different every time. But now, he's your hook and line and goddamned captain.

"I'm just saying." And your words ripple toward him. You'll have to wait to tell him your news.

"I got Jean breathing down my neck," he says. "I'm working sixty and we just got the new house. How the hell else am I supposed to relax?"

"Maybe you should worry more about living," you say.

"And what do you know about that?"

You've had a frayed string of boyfriends, and the last one you broke up with after you brought him to Jack and Jean's for dinner. The boyfriend came to your apartment off Sterling Highway, near the old fish processing plant, and limply held your hand as you walked to his truck. Your brother opened the front door—"Gracie," he roared and picked you up in a bear hug as if he were the only one who knew the weight of you. And you weren't surprised when your brother showed the boyfriend his new Winchester, ran his hand along the barrel and said, "I love this motherfucking country." You *were* surprised the boyfriend didn't make hunting plans with him, didn't talk skeet or clay or pigeon. And later that night, the boyfriend tells you, "Be gentle," when all you want to do is bite into his Adam's apple, because if there's one thing you know, it's that love is fierce. And then he says, "Is it just me, or is your brother a little off?" *Fuck you,* you say, and you know the boyfriend is right, so you get up and leave before he's right about you too.

Doormat gives a yelp and jumps up to set the hook. Hazmat pulls anchor and starts rowing, follows the king's run upriver.

"Don't you worry," Jack says. "Ours is coming." He reels in and checks his eggs, then douses them in his secret weapon—peppermint oil. "Sometimes the smell of king eggs with this reminds me of cod liver oil and earthquake stew," he says. "God, never again."

You taste it in your mouth and your stomach turns. You had a pantry full of naked, dented cans with serial numbers that your father, years before that, got cheap from the Good Friday Earthquake. When your mother ran out of groceries, she picked three cans and poured whatever was in them into a pot. Egg fu yung. Corn. Green beans. On a better day, one of the cans was ravioli. On a bad day, you let vegetables slip off your spoon on purpose, sending little waves to the edge of the bowl and back into the center.

"I visited Mom yesterday," you say.

"Good," he says.

"Don't you want to know how she is?" You're trying again and he's not having it. He hasn't been having it since he left for the navy right out of high school, and even before that.

"She's got you," he says. "Reel in. Something's on your line."

Your father worked as a juggy—put in seismic line for Western Geo, and he was gone a lot. Which was a relief. But you walked into your parents' bedroom looking to sneak some makeup and you saw he had taken red lipstick, something you don't remember your mother ever wearing, and in a hasty flourish written, "Sheila, I miss you already," at the bottom corner of the mirror on her dresser. Her name looped and trailed off with a comet's tail so "Sheila" read "Shield" if you hadn't known any better. You wondered how long the crimson wax had been there, proof, like a famous person's autograph, that, yes, she had seen him—he *had* been here. You could see she had washed the mirror and deliberately left it intact, a safety deposit of dust encased the letters. But there were cracks in the cursive, slight fractures where the glass glared right back at you.

Her cosmetics bag was filled with concealer and powder and beige bottles, and, while you rummaged for shadows and color, she walked in.

"That's mine," she said.

Your hand froze, your face already pale with what you had put on. And you looked at her and she looked down at the brown carpet.

"Don't," she said, quiet, and you knew you would never trespass again.

There's a rainbow trout on the end of your line—he's eaten all of your king eggs and he's small, about the length of a spoon.

"Child molester," Jack calls you.

"It's not my fault," you say.

The hook, made of surgical steel and meant for a fifty-pounder, has pierced through the jaw and gill. Dangling in the air, the rainbow looks like it's being used for bait. "I don't want you," you say to the ink-filled eye. You release him back into the river, but he might not make it. "He good as dead?"

"Never can tell," Jack says. "I was out here once, drifting by myself. I put in at Skilak, and it was calm at first, and then the wind picked up and made a mess of the water. Took me an hour or two to get to The Narrows, and by that time I needed to rest, so I let the current take me and swing me wide, beached me up at some marsh near Superhole." He stops to take a drink, a long one.

"And?" you say.

He's always had a stockpile of stories, things he's seen that get him new fishing buddies and free beers. "And I'm sitting there and I see a duck leading eight ducklings, they're all paddling behind her in a line, keeping close to the bank. Then an eagle flies in overhead, coming toward me and the ducks. All of a sudden, mama swims away from her brood and into the thick of the river, she's splashing and squawking and she's got her wing bent crooked like it's broken. The eagle swoops down with his feathers splayed back, talons going in for the kill, and I think she's a goner and right before he reaches her, she stops flailing and dodges out of the way and swims toward the bank.

That eagle looked confused, let me tell you. Flew away and landed on the top of a spruce tree and stayed there like he didn't know what the hell had just happened."

Doormat and Hazmat return and anchor up again near Eagle Rock. Half of the boulder is above the water—the tide is going out. They hold up a forty-five-pound hen, her belly bulging.

"Nice one," says Jack. "You going to give me some of those eggs? That's the tax for saving your spot."

"You give us some of that cure," says Hazmat. "And it's a trade."

"Fuckers," Jack says. "You know that's good cure. I get it sent from Oregon."

"You want eggs," says Hazmat. "We got to get something in return."

"What about that new jon boat you got for a steal because I knew the guy?"

"Shit," says Doormat. "How long you plan on using that against us?"

"As long as it takes," Jack says. "Tell 'em, Gracie."

"As long as it takes," you say.

For every story he tells, you think there's another one bubbling under the surface. He has stories about working on the slope in Prudhoe Bay, the circumpolar sun, as tall as a mountain, skating on the horizon, circling and circling. He says, "Some of the guys got shit-fucked in the head. Never slept—couldn't handle all the light, all the time. Started acting jumpy, like there was someone following them." You realized, a while back, that all his stories were about survival. "Me and this guy, Doodle, when we started to feel edgy, we'd tank a bunch of beers and then run our asses into the Arctic. There were only a few jerk-offs that could stand that ice water longer than me." He'll say,

"Did I tell you about joining the Polar Bear Club?" to some waitress or couple at the bar and Jean will roll her eyes at you, but you both let him talk—you both listen.

You feel the bump and turn, and the tourists are struggling against the current.

"If you can't row," Jack stands up and points, "take the outside channel. And stop banging my Willie."

"You know you like it," yells Doormat.

The tourists look confused until one leans over and whispers to the others and you know he's seen the Willie Boats decal on the side. They, and their matching blue jackets, head farther downriver.

"Fucking annoying," says Jack. "But I remember when I first came out here. I hit a few boats—thought maybe I'd get shot at."

"Tell the truth," you say.

"You're right," he says. "I rowed like a bastard. But I didn't want you to think I was good at everything."

"Don't worry," you say.

"I can't help it," he says.

One night, you woke up and he was dragging his mattress off the top bunk.

"What are you doing?" you said.

"Sleeping in the living room."

"Why?"

"Just because. I don't have to explain." He must have felt guilty for snapping at you because then he said, "How about I sleep near the door until you get used to that and then I'll move out."

You'd strain your eyes to make sure he was there. Or you'd hold your breath and quickly flick the flashlight on and off, hoping you wouldn't wake him, your eyes fuzzy with adjusting to the dark. And then the beam glared bright on carpet, and he was gone. But when your father came home, Jack would come back and put his mattress across the doorway so nothing could come in.

Your pole slams and he says, "Wait for it. Wait. Now." You grab the rod out of the holder and jerk back to set the hook, then do a double set.

"What you got there?" says Hazmat.

The pole is noodled into the river and the fish isn't moving.

"Check your drag," says Jack.

You can't reel in and he's not taking line.

"Pull up," he says.

"I am," you say.

"Let me see. You got a snag?" He takes the rod and lifts up. "That's a goddamn fish. And he's heavy as all hell. I can't move him."

You take the rod back and the reel creaks and the fish is taking line and you brace your feet. Then, pop, the line goes slack. "He's gone."

"Now you *have* to go into the river," he says. "You didn't do it with the last one and now look at what happened." He has rules: you have to take a dunk in the river after you lose a fish. You have to kiss the ones you catch.

"That's your thing," you say. "Not mine."

You lined up the empty cans on a shelf of snow, aimed the BB gun and fired.

You missed.

"Hold steady, look through the grooves," Jack said.

Your fingers felt the coldness of the trigger through your gloves. You hit the second and third and fourth, the tinny ring after each hit. You wanted the cans dead.

He put his hand on your shoulder. "Gracie, stop it," and he lifted the gun away.

You'd been eating earthquake stew for two weeks. That night, late, the two of you heard the back door open and close. You got up and the outside light was on and through the window, you saw your mother trudging away from the house, holding a gun. She wore her long-sleeved nightgown that went to her knees and black snow boots, her braid glistening with cold. She lined up six more earthquake cans and when one can was chock full of holes, she let out a puff of breath that froze in a moment of white. Then she stepped back with the gun at her side, and waited, her braid swaying across her shoulders. After a few seconds, she took aim at the next can. Two down. Then three.

Line zips out and you let it go longer this time.

"She's hot today," says Doormat.

You get the rod out of the holder and double set, yanking the tip high over your right shoulder.

"Careful," Jack says. "That's my favorite king rod."

The fish submarines straight across the river, line peeling out.

"Pull your anchors," Jack yells. "Get the fuck out of the way."

The king turns left and heads straight upriver.

"Hold on," he says, grabbing the oars. "We're going for a ride."

You and Jack sat in the living room, five empty ravioli cans in the middle of the floor. You paced around them, said the serial numbers out loud, backward. Trying to find the code for ravioli and sick of earthquake stew.

"It's no use," Jack said.

And that's when you both saw antlers, wide like trees, attached to a mountain of a moose.

He'd been watching you. Now you were watching him.

The two of you put on your jackets and went upstairs and climbed out the window onto the top of the awning. You leaned over the edge on your stomachs.

"Hey there, Grandpa," Jack said.

Grandpa had a black muzzle and a silver, scraggly beard. His antlers were shedding and you reached out to touch them—he let you. A piece of his velvet came off. You thought he might be hungry, that he'd like a piece of bread.

"We don't have any bread," Jack said. He suddenly sat up. "I think I know." Grandpa took a step back, but didn't leave. Jack went to the window and crawled back inside.

Grandpa breathed out a quick huff.

"I've got nothing to give you," you said.

He leaned back and lifted his front legs off the ground and made a nasally sound, calling a drawn "Noow, now, noooow."

"What do you want?"

He pushed off again, boxing the air. His hooves hit the ground. One two. One two.

"Gracie, I broke the code," Jack yelled. You put the velvet scrap in your pocket and hurried into the house.

Jack rows and you reel in line. He's fighting the current and you're fighting the fish, reeling in as you follow its path. And then the king turns, heads straight for the boat.

"Reel, goddamnit," he says. "Get rid of that slack."

You've got the butt of the rod jammed into your hip and you're hunched over, reeling as fast as you can.

"I still got him," you say, when you catch up and the whole weight of the fish tugs on the line.

"Pull up. Reel down," he says. "Pull up. Nice and slow."

Your arm and shoulder are worn out, but you hunker down, keep tension.

He drops anchor. "We'll fight him the rest of the way here."

You see the green metallic flash of the plug—the king is a couple of feet below.

"When you see the spin'n'glow, direct his head to me," he says.

The king dives, takes line.

"Let him take it," he says. "We got time."

Every inch you've gained is lost, and you're back where you started.

"Pull up. Reel down. There you go."

You don't want to tell him to take the rod, that your arm's about sapped. "Come on, you motherfucker," you say and dig in.

You see the plug, and follow the king to the bow of the boat. He dives again and you bury the rod in the water.

"What a shit," Jack says.

You circle the boat, switch places with Jack. Then you see the spin'n'glow, the shadow. "Lift," he says. He shoves the net into the water to bag him, yanks the handle up. Jack heaves the net into the boat and the king, the size of a small child, thrashes on deck. "Get the bonker," he says.

You look around, look in the stowaway, under the seat.

"For Christ's sake," he says. The king is slapping his tail against the deck and Jack kneels down on the net to hold him.

You hand him your thermos. "This is all we've got."

"Get me the knife then. We'll bleed him out." He stabs the gills, and he has to wrestle the fish to turn it over, and stabs again. Then he drags the body to the side and muscles the net back into the water, against the side of the boat, the current washing away a cloud of red.

"What a monster," he says. "Sixty-pound chromer, fresh as they get. He's still got sea lice on him."

"Jack," you say. You're finally going to tell him. "I got that job in Vancouver."

But you know and he knows that there's a difference between *got* and *took*, and you realize this as soon as you've said it.

Grandpa was in the yard—his antlers bobbing along with his bulky stride.

You found an old package of saltines and went outside, the snow swallowing your ankles and shins. You walked slowly and he didn't scare off.

"Are you hungry?" you said. You held out your hand.

"Here, you can have it." He was tall and big and beautiful. He moved a little closer and stopped.

"Gracie, move out of the way."

You looked behind and saw your mother holding a rifle. She had aim. But you were between her and Grandpa. "No," you said and he spooked. The thud of his hooves. You ran straight toward her and she sidestepped you and took one shot. But it was too late.

She raised her arm, ready to strike, and you winced—no one had ever hit you before. When you opened your eyes, she was pulling at her hair with both hands.

"Go inside," she said.

"I'm sorry," you said.

"Don't. I don't want to look at you. So go."

As you walked away you heard her saying the same thing over and over. "Give me the strength," she said. "Give me the strength."

You could see through the window as you went up the stairs. She sat in the snow, head bent forward, hands clasped behind her neck.

"Tell them about when you fell in love with a moose," Jack will say.

"We were starving and one came to our backyard and Gracie wouldn't let us shoot him."

"Alaska's in your blood," Jack says. "This is your home." He looks down at the king in the net. "What do you say, fish? Has she even thought about Jean and the kids?"

You start to say something, something like, "But what about making my own life?" and you stop. Your life has been made and unmade, your life is not your own. Once, the pastor of a church your mother dragged you to on Christmas and Easter said, "You were bought with a price," and you swear he was looking right at you. You wondered how anyone could be bought and owned and if you had any choice in the matter. You don't wonder anymore.

Jack lifts the king back onto deck. "You have to kiss him," he says.

"No," you say.

"You're the lucky one. I'm just fortunate. Don't mess with my fishing laws."

"I'm not going to kiss that fish." But you will, you always do.

When your father came home for the last time, the two of you found him on the couch. You tried to leave, but he woke up.

"It's been a while," he said. He sat up.

You didn't know what to say. Jack stepped in front of you.

"Your mom went out for a bit. Is that you, Gracie?"

You stood there, not answering.

"I know what'll fix us," he said. "How about I teach you some cards?"

You sat around the kitchen table. He shuffled and gave each of you five from the deck.

"Now there's the straight, the flush, the full house..."

That night you heard them fighting again, and Jack got up from his mattress near the door. "Stay here," he said.

And what happened, happened, and then your mother, with a swollen face that makeup couldn't cover, packed the two of you up and you left. But you wouldn't know the whole story until years later.

"That drunk bastard," Jack said. "He was hitting Mom and I tried to get in between them and then he got up in my face with a shotgun and said, 'You want to be a man? Let's see if you can act like one.' He points the gun at Mom and says I have to choose. 'Her or your sister. Who lives?' And I was pissing my pants, trying not to cry and he got right back in my face with the gun. 'Choose, you little piece of shit.' No, I said. He shoved me. I pointed at myself. I'll take it, I said. You let them alone. 'Pussy,' he says. 'I said choose.' Mom's standing there, doing nothing, hanging her head. And all I could think about was you, just a kid and all." He grabbed your arm. "I chose you, Gracie. Then he beat the shit out of me, told me who the fuck did I think I was, playing God?"

You drift downriver to Eagle Rock, and the tide has gone out, exposing a large chunk of the boulder.

"Show them your fish," he says.

You strain against sixty pounds, lift up the king.

"That's what I'm talking about," says Hazmat. He whistles.

"Charged so fast he had sea lice on him," Jack says.

"No fucking way," says Doormat.

"Tell 'em, Gracie."

"Covered all over," you say. "Looked like moss."

Jack puts the oars up. "Looks like we're going to call it a day, boys," he says and gets into a life jacket.

"Why do you need that?"

"Lose a fish . . . ," he says, and jumps into the river.

Everyone turns to watch you. He grabs the side of the boat and now you are someone who needs saving, an eagle diving into a mistake.

"I like your style," says an old fisherman in a camo vest.

Jack's up to his neck in glacial water, walking the boat, with you in it, toward the bank. And you, you're standing in a field of white, the crunch of snow beneath your feet. He wants you to tell him about the moon, but you tell him about the sun—it's big and bright and hovering on the horizon, the whole eye of it, circling. You run toward that gleaming hole, the point-blank end of the barrel, your arms in the air. Here, you wave. Pull the goddamn trigger.

But you reach the shore, take the keys, and get into the truck. He's sopping wet, but you stop at the bar on the way home. He tells a story or two, and you let him. Then you drive him to his house and when Jean sees you, she knows. "Help me punch out the rolls," she says, and when you're both in the kitchen, kneading dough, you understand that in the rise and fall of her hands she's saying, "Give me the strength." She's saying, "I can't do this alone."

US KIDS

Us kids smile and wave good riddance when Fox and Uncle Sly roll out one way and we roll another, bruised butts in the seats. We're piled into Big Mary, our station wagon that barely fits us all in and is a miracle for starting up. We're packed in with a huge pot full of frozen moose meat and whatever we have to eat in the back along with a jumbleball of afghans Polar Bear is always knitting. Fox and Uncle Sly go hunting at the homestead and Polar Bear drives us to see Aunt Sheila and Jack and Gracie, our cousins, at their house that Uncle Sly built all googly-eyed drunk. The house has gone through a few names—Slack Shack, Plywood Palace, and the one we all remember and still use is the Tiltin' Hilton.

Aunt Sheila has made gumdrop cookies and she sets a plate of them on the porch. We're pressed to see or taste any gumdrops but Kitty holds up hers. "I see a green one."

Polar Bear takes the pot and afghans into the house and we know to stay put outside. Aunt Sheila draws the curtains but we know what they're doing. Smoking and drinking homemade cranberry lick. We huddle near the side and listen through the cheap-cracked wood.

"The men are good and gone," says Polar Bear.

Ben signs to Rias so he can hear too. Jack shushes Gracie.

"Maybe they'll do us a favor and shoot themselves," says Aunt Sheila.

"Maybe," says Polar Bear. "I'll drink to that." There's the clink of bottles.

J.J. crosses his eyes and raises an imaginary bottle to his lips. Colleen, who has Baby T on her hip, laughs into her hand.

"They talk stars and moonlight in the beginning," says Aunt Sheila.

"And what we get is shit and moonshine," says Polar Bear. Another clink. A smash of glass on the floor.

Kitty gives out a yelp.

"Goddamnit," says Polar Bear.

We huddle closer against the house.

"I hear you out there," Polar Bear says. "You leave us alone. Scramola. We'll call you for dinner."

So we scram-ola. In front of the Tiltin' Hilton are two hills, one on each side because Uncle Sly had meant to put the house on one and the shitter on the other. "Nothing better than el-er-vation," he said. But he never got to it, built the house so it was some leaning wobbler between two piles of dirt. He didn't let Fox help him with the house. He did let Fox build the outhouse behind it, near the woods, and it's the only thing that stands up straight. But the hills are perfect for a game of Red Rover, and a rain has started up which puts the mosquitoes to bed for a bit.

" . . . we call J.J. over," and he comes mud-slipping down the hill to the arm-linked chain, but Rias and Colleen with Baby T on her hip keep hold. Gracie and Jack and Kitty come to the bottom and join J.J. and they make a wall. The others head up the hill.

" . . . we call Rias over," and because he might not see to lip-read with all the rain, J.J. draws an R in the air. Here slides Rias on his belly, and then he gets up and charges the line, breaking through the JackandGracie link. So he steals Kitty and now it's RiasandKittyandBenandColleenandBabyT at the bottom of the hill.

" . . . we call Gracie over."

Soon we're all mud creatures which is good because the rain stops and the mosquitoes wake up and swarm around us and the sun streaks through the shiner-eyed clouds.

"Dinner," yells Polar Bear, and she sees us kids all rolled and covered in mud. "Stay off the porch," she says. But she takes Baby T.

We settle on the gravel by the steps with our bowls of moose chili and for once there's something moose about it.

"Colleen, you make sure . . . everyone gets hosed . . . off . . . after everyone eats," says Polar Bear, swimming through her words.

A high-pitched-screaming-wail makes us all stop with our spoons. Aunt Sheila comes wobble-running around the Tiltin' Hilton. She steadies herself on the steps and sits down.

"What is going on?" says Polar Bear.

"There's a bird, or something, in the shitter," Aunt Sheila says, boozy and soft. "And it's trapped and it's dying and I pissed on it." She starts crying her face off. "We have to get it out. We just have to."

"For godssake," says Polar Bear. "It's a bird. What's it matter if the world's shy one?" She waves away the mosquitoes near her face.

"But it's alive," says Aunt Sheila. She's a crying mess.

"OK, OK," says Polar Bear. "Let's go take a look at this bird you pissed on."

"I didn't know it was down there," says Aunt Sheila.

We jump up and follow Polar Bear, the whole mud-covered line of us. Aunt Sheila trails behind, walking zigzag, and Ben falls back to help her.

Polar Bear turns around. "Sheila, that smell."

"I know," says Aunt Sheila.

The shitter smells like a shitter, even from a way off, because of the rain and because they ran out of lye a couple of days before and Uncle Sly kept forgetting to buy some.

Polar Bear gives Baby T to Colleen and goes in to take a look. "It's a dumb buzzard," she says. "That's all."

We take turns, plug our noses, and look down the hole that's surrounded in white Styrofoam so it's warm to sit on in winter. And because Fox made it, it's deep like he made our outhouse at the homestead. There's some flapping and some splashing and a hoarse-whistling-peep of a bird down there. But it's hard to tell what it is because it's dark in the shitter. We got a flashlight in Big Mary so Ben goes to find it and Polar Bear takes Baby T and Aunt Sheila back to the house.

"Promise me you'll get it out," Aunt Sheila says.

"They promise," says Polar Bear.

Ben shines the flashlight and our dried mud faces must scare the bird because it starts squawking. Not that the bird is much to look at either—covered in a slop of years of dirt and piss and shit.

"Get me a shovel," says Ben.

Jack goes to find one that's under the house. By this time we've breathed enough of the smell to get used to it and we've stopped plugging our noses. Ben has J.J. hold the flashlight as he leans in the hole with the shovel, but comes up quick.

"That's not going to do it," he says. "We need something to reach farther."

"I gotta go," says Gracie.

Colleen takes her and Kitty into the woods. Then she goes into the house and brings out a broom and a colander. "Polar Bear and Aunt Sheila and the baby are lying down," she says.

"We need tape," says Ben, and he and Jack and J.J. and Rias crawl underneath the Tiltin' Hilton to look for tape in the scattering of Uncle Sly's tools. Colleen holds the flashlight so Gracie and Kitty can look down the hole.

"He's crying," says Gracie.

"Little bird, don't you cry," sings Kitty.

"He's probably hungry," says Colleen.

Ben comes back holding a dusty roll of duct tape. It's late, but the sun just doesn't quit in July. The mud dries pale and cracked on our skin.

We tape the broom handle to the shovel and Ben holds J.J.'s legs as J.J. goes into the hole and Jack holds the flashlight.

"Pull me out," says J.J. "We need about this much more." He taps the tips of his fingers, uses his arm as a measuring stick. The shovel has reached the bird's head but we need to scoop him out.

"Get that rake," says Ben.

Rakebroomshovel is taped together.

J.J. goes in again, Ben has him by the ankles, and Rias funnels down the tool.

"Stop," yells J.J. "We're losing the shovel."

Ben motions to Rias who brings up the rake.

"Hold right there," says J.J. "I got to hold onto the shovel and you got to bring us both up."

The tape on the joint has come loose.

"Thing about smacked the bird in the head and then got me with it." There's a spot on his forehead where the dry-caked mud is scraped away. "Goddamn shithole."

We tape a stronger wrap.

"This is the last time I'm going," says J.J.

We get J.J. in and then the shovel and the rest.

"I got him," he says. "Pull up. Pull up." There's a squawk and a splash. "He jumped," says J.J. "The stupid bird jumped off." He peers down the hole. "I'm just trying to help you, you piece of shit."

"J.J., calm down," says Colleen.

He slaps the side of the outhouse.

Rias raises his hand.

"OK," says Ben. "You try."

We lower Rias, who is holding the end of the rakebroomshovel, into the hole. He gets the bird on, and we're lifting up, and we hear a bigger squawk and then nothing. The bird's not on the shovel because he's holding it, shit and all, close to his chest, both of them upside down. Ben gets Rias up close to the top and then lifts him and the bird straight up out of the hole. Jack grabs the bird and it's screaming and Rias stands up and takes the bird back, nesting it in the colander and cradling it in the crook of his arm. He pets it on the top of the head and if birds could smile, this bird would have been smiling you're-a-saint lovebeams at Rias.

"That's not a buzzard," says Colleen. "Look at the beak. That's an eagle. An eaglet."

"Still ugly," says J.J.

"Let's wash him up," says Colleen.

We fill a bucket of water at the pump. As long as Rias pets his head, the eaglet sitting in the colander lets us pour small cups of water over him. He's about the size of a chicken, with yellow feet, and yellow at the base of his hooked beak. With the slop off of him, his feathers are grays and browns with white spots on the fringe of his back. All in all, he could be mistaken for a scraggled patch of bear fur, and he wiggles off the water, ruffles up. We find a towel and Rias bundles him. Colleen brings over a half-eaten bowl of moose chili and hands the spoon to Rias.

"See if he's hungry," she says.

He is. He opens his beak and gobbles down the chili. Rias pets his head and then Kitty feeds the eaglet.

"Here you go, little bird," she says.

"Here you go, shitbird," says J.J. His voice pure syrup.

"Shitbird. Shitbird," chimes Jack.

And then Jack and J.J. chant together. "Shitbird. Shitbird. Shitbird."

"That's enough," says Colleen.

"He doesn't know what we're saying," says J.J. "Hey, pretty," he says. "Hey, ugly shit. See."

"Leave him alone," says Kitty. "He's just a baby."

We count and the eaglet sits in the colander on Rias's lap and eats eleven spoonfuls of chili.

"I want to keep him," says Gracie.

"We can't," says Colleen.

"We could teach him to hunt rabbits for us," says Jack.

"Or scratch people's eyes out," says J.J.

"What if he grew up big," says Kitty, "and we could ride him?"

"We'd go up in the sky," says Gracie. "To the mountains."

"You'd still smell the shitter up there," says J.J.

"We have to take him back," says Colleen.

There's a nest in the woods that's been abandoned for three years, but we figure the eagles must have returned, even if Jack says they haven't seen any flying over like they used to.

"Where else could this eagle have come from?" says Ben.

We march past the outhouse, into the woods, Rias carrying the eaglet and the colander. We stand at the base of a tall spruce tree, the tangled nest of branches up high, near the top.

"I see something," says Jack.

And then we all see a white spot of a bald eagle.

"They must be flying in from a different direction," says Ben.

There's no way we can climb the tree and put the eaglet back in the nest. He must have fallen or tried to fly or gotten pushed out, but how he got into the shitter, we don't know.

"We'll leave him here," says Ben. "His parents will hear him."

"But I wanted to keep him," says Gracie, and she buries her face against Rias.

"But he needs to be here, honey," says Colleen.

"I wanted to keep him too," says Kitty.

"But his family will miss him," says Colleen.

Ben gives the signal and Rias unwraps the eaglet and places him on the ground.

"Shouldn't we leave the colander?" says Colleen. "He seemed to like it."

Rias puts the colander on the ground and the eaglet jumps back into it. He strokes the feathers on the eaglet's chest.

"Say goodbye," says Colleen.

Kitty and Gracie kneel down next to Rias. "Goodbye, little bird," they say.

J.J. shakes his head at their sniffling.

Colleen grabs his arm. "Hush," she says.

We walk away, Rias the last one to leave. And when he does, the eaglet starts screeching and it's a good thing Rias can't hear him or anything for that matter or he'd turn back, and we pick up our pace, the sky falling blue through the trees.

We're all still a mudmess but we're tired.

"We'll sleep in Big Mary," says Colleen, so we don't get in trouble for being all mucked up in the Tiltin' Hilton. She sneaks inside and grabs the jumbleball of afghans. We put Gracie and Kitty in the front because they're small and the rest of us cram on the car floor and the seats and the hatch in the back. We pull the afghans over our heads to block out the light that's tricking us into staying awake.

In the late morning, maybe afternoon, we wake up because Jack gets up to go to the outhouse. Big Mary smells like Big Shit. We crawl out of the car dusty and cricked and yawning. No one says anything about what's in front of the porch. The house is quiet, except for the breeze of a snore we know is Polar Bear. What is there to say? J.J. throws a cup of water on Ben. And Ben chases after him. And we all get cups and throw water, splashing off the mud we've been wearing since the night before, dirty rivers trickling down to our toes. And what Polar Bear and Aunt Sheila see bleary-eyed, their hands raised against the glare of the sun, is us kids. Us kids laughing and running over a torn-to-pieces eaglet we bathed and fed and found this morning, brought back to us by birds or dogs or the upside-down nest of the world, stomping what we saved into the ground, an eagle buried under our feet, a flurry of feathers rising up.

THIS ONE ISN'T
GOING TO BE AFRAID

NAILS

She's nineteen years old and pregnant. She's nineteen years old and pregnant with me and waiting at the bus stop and it's fifty below in Fairbanks.

One of these times, she rides the bus to a job interview for a secretarial position. She and my father had twenty-three dollars to their name. "They wanted me to do a typing test," she says. "So right there I chewed off my fingernails—every one. I spit them into the trash can while the lady in the suit watched."

Now she keeps her nails long, just past elegant, and paints them blood-red to match her lipstick. Mine are like hers, so tough it hurts to clip them, but I keep mine short. There's the woman in red lipstick, sitting around the campfire, watching the sun slink down on Mount McKinley. A cigar glows in her mouth. She made the fire, swung an axe, and cut the spruce down to size. "And I didn't break a sweat," she says. She fans out her fingers over the flames. "Or a nail."

BICEPS

We went fishing on the Russian River with aunts and uncles and cousins. The salmon were running, too fast we joked, because no one was getting any hits on their line. The bank, about five feet higher than the riverbed, dropped off into rocks and shallow water—first inches and then deeper as you moved farther out.

My mother took a turn, and cast her line, let the line drift a ways with the current. The rod bobbed with a bump—"Fish On! Fish On! Colleen's got a Fish On!"—and the line paid out. We had four other lines in the water and quickly reeled them in. A bunch of zippers coming frantically undone—that's the sound. The fight began and the pole nodded down and up. She reeled, let the fish run, reeled some more.

We waited. She fought. And the salmon broke through the surface, thrashing against the current. He was a big, fat, bullet of a fish. She yanked and the salmon flew through the air and flopped with a violent smack on the rocks. "Go get him," she yelled. My cousin Jig scrambled for the net but then the swim-crazed fish snapped the line. She saw what we saw—the salmon dancing toward freedom—ditched the pole, slid down the bank, and crashed toward the fish in her waders. Tackled him down and threw him over her head toward us, but he leapt back toward the water. She dove again, and the fish slipped out of her hands. "You piece of shit," she said and jumped after him, wrestling him to the ground. Took five heave-hos before she tossed him up on the bank. Jig bonked him on the head with a rubber mallet until he wasn't moving. She flexed her biceps for the boys. "When you got these you don't need a net," she said. Behind us, the Fish and Game warden stood, arms crossed, head bent in laughter. "I ain't never seen anything like it," he said. What he meant, I know, was that he had never seen anybody like her.

CALVES

My mother drove a gold station wagon when I was younger—the brassy paint a loud announcement when I craved invisibility. But she loved that car, even if it didn't handle snow too well. There's this time on Old Seward Highway and we were humming along to soft rock oldies in the weekender traffic heading back to Anchorage. We'd visited my aunt Kitty in Sterling, snagged a few reds for the freezer, had a girls' night out. And then a loud clang, like a pot lid hitting the kitchen floor, interrupted "When a Man Loves a Woman." This had happened before. She swerved into the emergency lane, parked, and jumped out, leaving her door open. The roar of passing trucks drowned out my yelling at her. I slunk down in my seat as she looked left and then ran across the lanes in her red high heels, her calves sharp angles of muscle. She waved at the traffic that honked at her, gave one man in a white Ford the finger, then picked up the hubcap. Hugging it to her chest, she made her way back. "What an asshole," she said as she slammed the door shut. When we got home, she used her red heels to kick the hubcap back on.

SHOULDER

She went on a hike in the woods with her father and brothers to scout out moose. She carried a rifle about as tall as she was and later Ben took it because the gun was heavy. Her father told them to climb and sit on the tree stand. He would come back for them when the sun hit the ridgeline. She and Ben sat on the stand and waited. They didn't talk. She let her legs hang over the edge.

"Did you hear that?" Ben whispered.

All she heard was trees.

"I know I heard something."

She tried to see how far she could hang off the edge, facedown, before she felt like falling.

"Stop that. You'll knock your head off," he said.

She didn't fall, but her hat did. She went to climb down the stand and Ben grabbed her arm.

"Don't go down there."

But she twisted until he let go and she climbed down. She retrieved her hat and put it back on her head—then a growl came from the woods. She got knocked to the ground. She says, "One thing you learn, along with shooting, is how to play dead." She held her breath and covered her face with her hands. There were gunshots. There were shouts. Her body rolled. She felt pressure on her left shoulder. Then she saw Ben.

Ben held her under her arms and dragged her to the base of the tree.

"You got to climb. The bear might come back." Ben's eyes were wired open.

He stood her up and placed her hands on the wood footings. Everything looked smaller and clouded and everything smelled rotten. She climbed her way up the stand with Ben behind, pushing and shoving. Her shoulder throbbed, as if it suddenly remembered what had happened, and Ben wadded up his flannel shirt and tried to stop the bleeding.

When she's visiting me in California, she'll wear a tank top and people will ask about the puckered scar on her shoulder. She'll say, "I got mauled by a grizzly in Alaska." And they believe her. They believe Ben fired the rifle and they believe she climbed back up the tree onto the stand, blood seeping from the wound. The hook digs in deep and then she'll say, "Actually, it was an accident. I snagged my shoulder on a metal spring while hiding under the bed." They chuckle with relief. "Man, you had me going." Kids and a game of hide-and-seek. But they don't ask what she was hiding from. The truth is there are grizzlies and there are fists and bottles and belts. There are choices: play dead or hide.

HANDS

There were bets, when she said she was getting married, on how long it would last. One week. Two months. She was seventeen and still in high school and he was twenty. "We were two podunk kids in Alaska," she says. When my father went to ask for her hand, the conversation was brief. He went into the garage where her father, Fox, was fixing his truck.

"Sir, I'd like to marry your daughter."

"Which one?" Fox held screws between his lips.

"Co—"

"Oh, I know which one." Fox kept on with the monkey wrench. The sound of tinkering went on for a long while. "You still standing there?" he said. "Hand me a flat head."

My father waited and then Fox said, "Well, if you can feed her you can have her." And my grandmother figured a man who borrowed a gun and cleaned it up real good before returning it couldn't be all that bad, so she and Fox signed the consent form because my mother was under age. At the ceremony, my father put a borrowed wedding band on her finger. He was twenty and couldn't afford to buy one.

My mother wears a ring now topped with a boulder of a diamond and calls herself a "sparkling bitch." Every one of her fingers has a wide inner tube of a knuckle, an obstacle a ring has to fit over. Both of her pinkies are crooked—boomerangs she says—breaks that weren't allowed to heal properly. Her sisters have the same hands. Her brothers have worse—they are missing tips and parts of fingers. They all have stories full of funny accidents and slips and remember-whens, and they laugh about it, but their hands tell a darker truth.

FEET

"I can hear it in your voice," my mother says. "You're disappearing."
She's visiting me in Bakersfield and we sit on the concrete in my backyard smoking vanilla cigars, feet in the pool.

She's going to tell me how they all had to clear land—they felled
spruce trees and chopped them up and stacked the wood. They dug
up roots and dragged rakes over the hard-packed dirt. And there were
rocks. "We made piles and piles. For days all we did was shovel up
rocks. I remember looking up at the sky and it was going to storm.
There was lightning flashing in the distance. I told the big man up
there—you take lightning to that branch above me and send it crash-
ing down, knock me out, because I'm not doing this anymore. But he
didn't listen. All he gave me was some pittering rain. So I went behind
the shed, raised the pickax, took it to my foot. I sat on the porch in a
bandage—no more rocks." My mother leans back on the heel of her
hand and I brace myself for the punch. She says, "You don't know
what you can endure."

I asked Uncle Benny about it. "Did she really pickax her foot?"

"No," he said. "That was J.J. But it could have been any one
of us."

SKIN

Bathing was a production. First, Ben soaked in the water, lathered
up and rinsed. Then her. Then J.J. Then Rias. Then Kitty. And so on
down the line, oldest to youngest. The people changed—the water
didn't. The order reversed, youngest to oldest, the next week. On a
good day, the water was lukewarm. On a bad day, she got into the tub
and the water was gray, cold, and filmy. She said, "Maybe that's why
we all have good skin. That and having to choke down a spoonful of
cod-liver oil every day."

She looks at least ten years younger than her real age. And she knows it. I learned to anticipate the questions before they were asked. "Yes, really. Not my sister. My *mother*." She jokes that we'll be senior citizens together—that eventually our age difference won't matter anymore, that we'll be two of the same person. I think of years passing and see myself grow old and wrinkled, while my mother stays young because she's told time to leave her the hell alone and it wouldn't dare disobey.

TEETH

She went ice-skating on the pond at Huffman Elementary. They were playing tag and she was *it*. She chased after J.J. in his blue-striped scarf. He skated faster and faster and she followed, reached out with her hand and right before she got to that scarf she hit a chink in the ice and fell, smashed her face.

She lost some blood, and half of a front tooth, but her mother didn't take her to get it fixed. A chipped tooth was useful—with the sharp edge she cut fishing line and thread. But her mouth swelled up, her lips. "Then I got a fever and green shit started coming out of my nose and gums," she said. When her temperature was 103, her mother took her to the doctor and the doctor yelled because the infection was spreading toward her brain. "If you had waited any longer," he said. "She would have died."

Her brothers called her Snaggletooth, but she didn't cover her mouth with her hand when she laughed. "Those fuckers. I smiled more, just to spite them."

At fifteen, she started working at an ice cream shop in the Dimond Mall. My father was working there as a janitor and one day he saw her, wanted to know who that girl was with *that* smile. Over the years, she tried to get the tooth repaired. Crowns wouldn't fit, and always the base was black and unhealthy. Right before she turned forty-five, she finally got a crown that looked like a normal tooth. "I told that damn dentist that I wanted my teeth to look like snow bricks in an igloo." My uncles still call her Snaggletooth, say it's still there, underneath.

EYES

We went to the homestead for Thanksgiving. Thirty people crammed into a one-room cabin with a wood stove. Uncle Benny made seafood chowder in a pot you could bathe in. The secret, he tells me, pour the bacon grease in with the whipping cream. The adults played pinochle, one game on each end of the table. I picked up my mother's stack and arranged them by suit—she'd let me even though I'm cursed at cards. She'd look at her hand and say, "No marriages, just like Ben," and he'd say, "Fuck 'em and leave 'em." They drank Carolans Irish Cream and homemade cranberry lick from the bottles, passing them down, sip after sip.

She stepped outside and I went with her. She was a little tipsy, happy-tipsy. We turned to the back of the homestead, arms linked, headed toward the outhouse. The clear night strewn with ice-picked stars. We were trudging along in the snow and stopped. Above the ridge, serpentine green ribboned the sky, tangled and bright. I'd never seen them—neon streamers making love to the darkness and I couldn't stop looking.

I haven't seen them since. But that color, that electric green, she carries with her. It's in her eyes when she's telling me that I don't understand, telling me about scouring the house on Bragaw Street with Ben. "Ben and I went for so long without dinner. It must have been months. There was a closet upstairs. When Fox came back from Korea he hid old K rations and twenty-pound bags of oranges in the crawl space behind the closet. Late at night, Ben and I'd sneak back there like rats." I didn't want to believe this story. Sure, they were poor and there were five children and one on the way and sometimes they didn't have enough food. But, growing up, she and Ben pissed the bed and, as punishment, they didn't get dinner. I didn't want to believe that she ate K rations and rotten oranges, and I didn't want to believe her when she said, "I got so skinny my hair fell out." And then, when I didn't say anything, she laughed. "A goddamned bald rat. So fuck you."

STOMACH

"I was pregnant with her all winter. God, I was fucking depressed. We were living in Fairbanks then and all that darkness, thought I was going to lose my mind. The only thing that I could keep down was ice cream, so I ate my way through gallons. Turned into a fat ass, which made me more depressed. And then—" She points at me. "She was this dinky little thing that only weighed about five pounds." But she blames me for the sprawling stretch marks on her stomach. Tells everyone that I took a shit inside the womb. "And she's been giving me shit ever since," she says and winks.

My father told me that she didn't know what to do with me at first, that she held me like she was holding a shotgun. She'd throw me up too high in the air. "This one," she'd say to him, "isn't going to be afraid of anything."

CHEEKBONES

She has her mother's and grandmother's bone structure. My face has a roundness, has two half-moons, where they have chiseled features. Ice Queens, I call them. I imagine they were once glaciers, hard and melting, split by a fist that came down from the clouds. In one photograph of the three of them, they have braided hair at the napes of their necks and are standing next to a 130-pound halibut hanging up on a hook, its broad, white belly as wide as a tablecloth. A line of black bass and ling cod lie dead in front of their fishing boots. My mother and grandmother and great-grandmother smile wide, smile with their whole bodies, but to me, their bones speak a louder truth. They say: We are stronger than you.

POINT MACKENZIE

RIAS

In the woods of the homestead. On my back. Snow falls and hills on me. Here it's like when I close my eyes and hold my breath in the tub. No one finds me in the snow. No one tells me to chop wood, to pick up rocks, to check the traps. No one points to their lips, moves them slow, right in front of my face. And then the whole wide ground goes slap-punch under me. I run to the cabin. Ben is there. A plane, he says. He makes his hand into a plane, flies it across his face, and then the plane falls. Crash, he says, then he spells it. Over there. He points to the swamp. Fox went to see, he says. Fox comes back and tells us not to go over there. Three dead. No fire.

Fox is mad. He's mad a lot. But he tells us to chop wood and it's cold. There's a hole in my boots. They used to be Ben's. My hands are cold. All the sky is cold. I act like I don't know what Fox says. He gets in my face and Ben is there too. We are all there. Me, Ben, Fox, and J.J. Not the girls. Colleen and Kitty are in the cabin with Polar Bear. Fox is red in the face. With Polar Bear, Ben lips P.B. and I know to hide the gumdrops he took, know to run up to her fast and stop the red in her face. But there's no way to stop Fox. He makes Ben tell me. Ben says, Rias we have to. And then spells with his hand. W-o-r-k.

Fox says a thing to me. I know it's bad. I know this by the way he lifts his hand up and Ben steps in. Fox hits Ben and Ben is on the ground. There is blood on his nose and blood on the snow. Fox walks out. I ask Ben what Fox said. M-o-t-h-e-r-f-u-c-k-e-r? What is motherfucker? I know fuck. And fucking moron. Fox, he says, is one. Not you. He says, like a mean fuck. Got it? Yes, I nod. But Fox is not a mother. I spell f-a-t-h-e-r-f-u-c-k-e-r. Ben laughs for a long time. I try to make him laugh as much as I can. His mouth opens and God is there.

Fox drives away to find help. He says to leave the crash be. That we don't steal.

A snowstorm comes in and we can't go see the crash if we want to. Polar Bear lets us eat snow in a bowl with milk and vanilla after we eat stew. Kitty plays and feeds me from her spoon. Colleen and J.J. and Ben don't let her do it to them. If I don't, she cries. And she throws things on the floor. And Polar Bear takes the bowl away. But not this time. We eat all of it and then drink the rest that melts. Ben looks out at the white. He writes his name on the glass. I write mine. Out there is the plane, but we can't see past the porch. I took a plane to school. I was gone a long time. I had to learn to sign and spell and talk. Ben asks me what it was like in a plane. I tell him I am a bullet. I got shot to Texas. He draws a gun and then a neck and head that sticks out of the gun. Then he wipes it off before Polar Bear sees.

We wake up and Colleen and Polar Bear make breakfast. Us boys cut and chop wood while Fox is gone. J.J. throws down the axe and heads to the swamp. Ben runs to him. I go too. Ben grabs J.J. but J.J. never follows what Ben says. So we all go to the swamp. There are pieces of metal on the snow and trees broke off. Wires. A bag that isn't hurt. J.J. opens it before Ben can stop him. Just a look, says J.J. A blue sweater is on top. He shows us. Woman things, says Ben. Ben walks in front. Far. I see him step down. He gets up after a time. Walks back to J.J. and me. He has that I-saw-something-bad look. We have to go back, he says. Now. J.J. shakes his head. Ben drags J.J. in the snow and gives up. I go with Ben.

What did you see, I ask. Rias, not now, he says. Tell me, I say. Nothing, he says. Tell me, I say. It was nothing, OK. But I know it's not the truth. I look back for J.J. but I don't see him. We go to the cabin and Polar Bear comes out. Her mouth is open. Big. I can't get the red out of her face this time, I know. She yanks our arms and starts in on Ben. All I can do is wait for her to be done. I hold her arm, but she's strong. My throat feels like a chunk of ice. That's what it feels like when I try to talk. She stops and there's J.J. with the blue sweater. And he has a leash in his hand. But then at the end of the froze-stiff leash is a shiny collar, and what we are all stopped for is the dog head. A cut-off head. Frozen. Curly. Mouth open. Pink tongue. He's walking a dead dog head. Polar Bear runs off the porch and now J.J. gets it.

But then she runs up the porch to me. She is right in my face. Zacharias, did you make J.J. take the dog? He says you did. I look at Ben. Then I look at J.J. His eyes say please. I don't think fast enough. No, I say. I should say it was me. She yells at us. She opens her mouth and God is not there. Ben takes me into the cabin. We eat oatmeal. The girls stare. I ask Ben what kind of dog. Ugly. He spells p-o-o-d-l-e. Kitty grabs at Colleen's leg. I let Kitty put curlers in my hair so she won't cry.

COLLEEN

Kitty grabs at my leg and starts to cry when we hear Polar Bear yelling and hitting J.J. So I tell her to play with her curlers and she puts them in Rias's hair. Polar Bear won't cut his hair because it's so pretty and dark and curly. He looked like a little girl when he was a baby. My baby, if I was old enough to have one. When the plane hit, I was in the cabin doing dishes and I swear to God, I thought we were having another earthquake like the big one that happened when we were living in a trailer off Old Seward and I was holding Rias's hand and Polar Bear was holding Kitty and almost fell over.

I ask Ben what happened but he won't tell me.

Polar Bear comes back inside and says, "Get out."

So I put a hat and coat on Kitty and we go outside. Polar Bear's been telling us to get out a lot, and I know when she does that, we can expect another Kitty sometime soon, and she's been eating more too.

J.J. is sitting on the deck, hunched over his knees, his face shoved into the crook of his elbow. "You OK?" I ask. But he doesn't say anything. I know to leave him alone when he's crying and he doesn't answer right off because he just gets madder. I look up at Ben and Ben shrugs. Something's going on with the boys and no one's giving it up.

Kitty whines on my arm. "Leen, I wanna make snow angels."

So I take her hand and help her off the porch and we walk in the snow, slow, because she's little, and her boots are too big. I put extra socks on her but it doesn't matter. She's got to grow into them.

Kitty sings, "Snow angels, snow angels." Ben and Rias make them too. I'm swishing my arms in the snow for wings and keeping my eye on J.J. in the distance and it hurts my neck. He's crying it out. But if you asked him he'd say he isn't crying. He says he might be getting sick. Or his eyes don't like the cold. But I see him get up, open up the door real quick, reach to the left, and come out with his .22. I bet Polar Bear's on her bed with a pillow over her face and didn't wake up to see who's there. J.J. starts marching off in the snow. "Where's he going?" I ask Ben.

"Traps," he says.

I get up and brush the snow off me. I make Kitty stay with Ben and Rias. It's one of those misty snow days, a breath of fog every place you look. "J.J., wait," I say. He doesn't look back at me. Acts like he can't hear. But I'm fast and he hears me running and he starts running through the woods. Shithead. My lungs are filling with rocks. "J.J.," I yell. All I hear is quiet and the humming of the fog.

Then there's a gunshot, and I figure J.J.'s got something because he's the best shot out of all of us. So I walk a hitch faster to try and find him and then I hear him. "Holyfuckingpieceofshit," he says. There's another gunshot. And I see his black hat and his back's to me and I see a dot of red up ahead of him. Something makes me stop, not tell him I'm there watching. His gun is on the ground and he's got a rabbit, white in its winter coat, and he steps on the head and yanks the feet and the body goes one way and the head stays there under his boot and there's blood. And he keeps saying "Holyfuckingpieceofshit, holyfuckingpieceofshit" and he stomps and stomps on the head. He grabs the legs and then pulls all the fur and skin off inside out and tosses the skin on the ground. He digs in his pocket and takes out his knife and makes one slash on the belly and then swings the legs up over his head like a lasso and guts are flying out. I've seen moose gutted and deer but there's something about the way he keeps saying "holyfuckingpieceofshit."

"J.J.," I shout.

He stops and turns around. "What do you want?"

"Come on," I say. "Let's get that cooked up and see if Fox is back."

"How long you been standing there?" he asks.

"I just came up on you."

"I got him twice in the head," he says. "Target practice."

He picks up his gun and the skin and walks ahead of me and one boot makes prints tinged with red until we get into the thicker snow and our legs are swallowed up.

J.J.

I think they're diamonds on the collar and the dead people didn't need them anyways anymore on account of them being dead and all and rich because they ride in planes and we're always having to eat oatmeal and moose liver and rabbits if we can get them but for Thanksgiving the other day we ate moose steak and last Christmas all we got for a present was Rias coming home and nothing else. Ben tells me to look out for something we can use and then he stands there and lets me take all the blame and Rias is the only one who doesn't get it so bad. And Kitty. But all Rias had to do was nod his head and maybe then Polar Bear wouldn't have gone to fits on me because she sure doesn't go to fits on him as far as I've seen. Holyfuckingpieceofshit. She pushes me and I'm on the ground and she takes the frozen leash and hits me with it and all I'm thinking is how she thinks she's hurting me and she's not because of my big coat but the sound is loud so it sounds like she's hurting me. Then I'm thinking of what it must look like with Polar Bear holding this leash and this icy poodle head swinging around and I wish I wasn't facedown in the snow pretending so I could see how funny it is. I bet she looks like some crazy and then she tells me to stand up and I rub my eyes so it looks like I've been crying and then she knocks me in the face. Holyfuckingpieceofshit can she hit hard when she wants and I can take it anywhere else, but not my face. I don't have to pretend anymore and she tells me to get rid of the dog and wrap it up in the burn pile and I better not let Kitty see it but I don't know what she did with the blue sweater Holy—

Colleen comes up and I've got the rabbit cleaned up good and we walk back to the cabin and when we get there she takes the rabbit and starts chopping it up with onions and potatoes and Polar Bear is gone and Colleen says she must be walking out for a bit like she does sometimes.

KITTY

snow angels snow angels you sing rias and ben shake his head and rias you say kitty and he talk and he sound funny and i laugh and ben is mad you sing ben and he not listen to me you cocksucker and ben say don't talk like that kitty ok you remember when i hurt my finger and it bleed you remember and ben say yes i got in trouble when you hurt your finger and there j.j., and leen and j.j. has a rabbit and it bleed and i put snow on rias you eat it and he open and it gone and i put more snow and there mama

BEN

Polar Bear comes walking up while we're making snow angels with Kitty, arms full of stuff from the crash. "Go get Colleen and J.J.," she says. So I go find them in the cabin and we're all looking at her and she says, "We're going to go get some things, things we can use around here. And if you tell Fox so help me God." She has that belt-and-bawl warning in her eyes and if anyone told Fox, we'd all get it. Her too. Her the most. A while back I was chopping wood behind the homestead, we'd come in from Anchorage for some moose hunting, and she had kicked us all out, told Colleen to boil some water for a bath. I wasn't spying or anything, was clearing out some of the trees and the curtain covering the window fell. That's when I saw her, just her back, covered in smokecloud bruises, more smoke than skin. She turns around and I duck, dive into the snow. When I look up the curtain is hanging again. I know I've had bruises like that, but it's something different seeing them on someone else.

"Walk in a line," says Polar Bear. "So there's only one trail of tracks." We don't take the bags, just things here and there so Fox won't know. Fox said there were three bodies and I'd already seen the dead woman when J.J. and Rias and me hiked to the crash the first time. Polar Bear points to three different mounds of snow. "Stay away from those," she says. J.J. leans over to me. "So help me God," he mouths.

J.J.

I whisper "So help me God" to Ben and he smiles and Polar Bear is always saying that but the only thing I think he's helping her with is knocking the shit out of us and I don't get why she gets mad at me for the dog collar and blue sweater and now we're all ransacking the crash. She took the sweater from me and must have kept it, must have thought about it, how these people are froze-fuck dead and don't need sweaters or anything else for that matter and maybe God did help us. Maybe God took his big fat hand and grabbed the plane and crashed it right here just so we'd find it, and I'd find this buck knife, sharp as shit, not rusted up like the one I've been using, and put it in my pocket, and the next time Rias snitches on me like he did, I'll take it out, tell him if he ever does that again I'll cut his good-for-nothing ears off, nail them to a tree. That'll show him, and I could tell Fox that we stole. "Nothing fucking worse than a thief," he says. "Or taking handouts." I'll tell him and that'll show Polar Bear, but then we'd all be in trouble and then Polar Bear would have it out for me and I don't know who's worse, her or Fox.

COLLEEN

Polar Bear says it's time to go back and she's biting her lip and I can tell she's feeling sick. It's getting dark and it's starting to snow again which is good because it will cover our tracks. Kitty starts to whine "Leen, Leen," and I know she won't stop until I pick her up so I do. And I've got all this stuff in my hands. I found some clothes, a jacket, found some butterscotch candy, kicked up by our walking, like it had come down with the storm. I knew what it was right away, butterscotch is Fox's favorite and we only get it around Christmas, if that. I gave Kitty a piece and for once she smells like something other than syrup and shit, which is what all little kids smell like. And what I've got stashed in my boot is a bottle of perfume I found. How the glass didn't shatter in the crash I don't know, but I made sure Polar Bear didn't see. Because if she had she would have taken it for herself. I'm going to hide this bottle, take it out whenever I need to smell something besides dirt and smoke and rabbit stew. Or maybe I'll pour it in the stew, maybe it'll clean us all from the inside out, make Polar Bear stop being sick, fix Rias's ears, get the dark looks out of J.J.'s eyes. Or I'll drink it all myself, see if I don't up and glow so hot and coal-bright everyone just leaves me alone, never asks me to do anything ever again. Polar Bear has us pile the stuff on the porch and tells us to go inside while she hides it, will bring it out bit by bit when Fox is gone working the slope so he won't notice. She's been gone a long time and we're waiting for her to come back so we can eat dinner.

KITTY

leen pick me up you hurry up right now and leen run fast and there outhouse and there a noise and mama there and blood and leen say don't look and my eyes dark is mama ok and leen run and say shhh yes can you keep a secret i promise i promise and mama sleep and we eat stew and the door open and fox home remember boom and you run outside how come and leen say the plane crash and i sit on leen you be mama and i be baby and you be bird and i be . . . and leen say chick nooo i be cake and leen say kitty you can't be cake and ok you be stove and i be cocksucker and leen say don't ever say that again and fox laugh and leen say i'll put soap in your mouth and fox pick me up and in my ear he say now say motherfucker and i say motherfucker and fox laugh big

BEN

Colleen tells me to take J.J. and Rias to check the traps, and we don't need to, and it's snowing and dark, but there's something in her face that I know means don't-ask-questions. When we get back to the cabin, Polar Bear is sleeping and we eat rabbit stew and deal out the cards and play slap-queen with the lantern turned down low. Then Fox comes home, says he had to spend the night at some station because of the storm, says they're going to come get the bodies from the crash in the morning. I have a night of sleepkillers where I dream and walk miles and miles in my head but I feel it everywhere. Like my body went out without me and got its sorry ass ran over by a truck and then came back. In one, I'm walking the swamp again with Rias and J.J. and J.J. is making noises, making fun of the way Rias sounds. J.J. is honking like a goose and I turn to tell him to quit it but he's not there and neither is Rias. I yell at them and tell them we should go back and then I step into a ditch and she's there, the dead woman. Her clothes are shredded and her tit is hanging out and I look away. But I remember. She's lying on her side, her arm broke and bent in a way it shouldn't be. Her ear is gone. There's a gash and blood on the side of her head and it's trickled and dried down her face and there's a little on the snow. Sometimes I run and see the blue sweater from the bag of woman things that J.J. found and I cover her up instead of what I did which was kick snow on her really fast so she wouldn't be so naked and then get out of there. I didn't want Rias or J.J. to see. Sometimes I fall into the ditch and she's there and when I turn to run there's ten of her surrounding me in a circle. Their mouths are frozen open, but not like they're screaming, like they were just about to say something and then they died. This other time, I go back looking for her and I can't find her and I walk for hours and it's getting dark and I think I see my own footprints and I follow them. But they go the wrong way. When I can't walk anymore I find her. I take off my jacket and cover her because the blue sweater isn't there anymore and all I can think about is how I'm going to be in trouble for losing the jacket because I can't say how I was out by the crash and gave it to her. But what I can't understand is how Fox left her like that. He had to have seen her. Sometimes I walk and everything is falling soft for a spell and I know she would have liked to be where I am at that moment, when a hush comes down with the snow. And sometimes I talk to her. Sometimes she talks back.

RIAS

The men go to the crash. They take the plane and what was in it. Snow falls where the crash was. But there is a scar there. I felt it when the plane hit. Hard. And there are trees smashed. It will never look like it did. But trees move. In the wind and in storms and God is there. Some things move and some things are dead. Some things I can't tell yet. Polar Bear yells even when her mouth is closed. So does Fox. Kitty moves and moves. But she slows up as she gets big. Colleen moves and she thinks no one can see. J.J. is scared to move. Ben moves too much and gets hurt. When I leave for school and come back, I have to learn them as if they were new to me. Learn their lips when they talk. Their hands and eyes. I fly in a plane and to them it's like I crash down.

I don't know if I move. So I hold my breath.

MINERS AND

TRAPPERS

Your sister-in-law Jean calls you because Jack has been gone for too long—one night she can understand, one night means he's passed out drunk at Good Time Charlie's or at his buddy Butch's or Chako's again and he always comes stumbling back, either by himself or because you've gone and driven him home. He's never been gone past noon the next day, and she knows this is your day off and the roads are bad, but he's probably dead and she has to keep pretending for the kids and, "You have to find him, Gracie. You have to find him and bring him home and I can't call the police and I can't ask anyone but you and I love him and I don't know why but I need you to." You tell Hyde that you have to go pick up Jack.

"You're not going out in this," says Hyde, like he always does—the two months since he's moved in.

"I have to," you say.

"Let me drive then," he says.

Your brother has told you on many occasions that Hyde is a "pussy-whipped fuckshit" and that you better not end up with him. In other words, Hyde is the kind of man that is sewing you a miniskirt out of a pair of his old Carhartts for the Miners and Trappers Ball at Fur Rondy in Anchorage. In *other* other words, Hyde is a kind man. Jean gave you her old sewing machine and you said, "What am I supposed to do with this?" You and Jack, well, the only things you know how to mend are fishing lines tied to sharp hooks.

You grab the keys from Hyde. "Someday you're going to have to say no," he says.

"Someday," you say.

It's, as Jack says, Fucking February, when everyone goes crazy and shoots themselves in the head. Jean locks up his guns from Christmas to Easter, Baby Jesus to Dead Jesus to Just Kidding Jesus. You and Hyde go to church with Jean and the kids every other Sunday. You know that the both of you don't fill in the gap that should be Jack sitting beside her. But he says fishing is his religion, the river is his sort of god—will drown the shit out of you, an eagle, or a goddamn mosquito, and it makes no difference, and nothing is half-assed. Days like this you tend to agree with him: when it's ten below and you'd sell your right arm to chug a few bottles of cheap wine that would knock you out long enough to forget it's winter, and to forget you decided to stop drinking four days ago after taking a pregnancy test that Hyde may or may not know about. He's been acting a little too concerned lately and hinting at the future with words like "someday" and you know if you tell him he's going to stick forever because he's been wanting to get married for a year already and, yes, he's the first guy you've been with that didn't make you want to see how far you could push him. But, is that enough? To marry someone because he doesn't make your stomach queasy with that "Baby, baby I need you" look that means you could tell him to eat fish guts and he'd do it? Hyde wouldn't. But he thinks everything happens for a reason. He is usually happy and in a good mood so there must be something wrong with him. He's a goddamn optimist. He's a morning person. He hums in his sleep.

The first place you always check is Good Time Charlie's and they have a phone in the back office, but no one answers it, no one can hear it over the strip pole music. In the summer, Jack might be passed out in the parking lot, sleeping in his truck. In the winter, Sasha might have let him sleep in the office behind the bar she tends because she went to high school with him and has, you suspect, always been in love with him. You think it is only a matter of time before Jack mixes up his seasons and goes out to his truck to sleep it off in the middle of winter and freezes to death. He did once, but Sasha found him and dragged him inside.

Good Time Charlie's is a strip club that used to have the best fish 'n' chips in town which you know because Sasha would give you an order to go while you were rounding up Jack. But Charlie died along with the "no one knows but it's not beer" batter recipe. And there was sawdust on the floor until one day it was gone, and Sasha told you that the strippers had threatened to quit because G-strings and sawdust don't mix, you can imagine. Before that, before the sunken line of the roof, Good Time Charlie's was a bustling place back in the oil days, the pipeline days, the "let's conquer the frontier" days. There are tinted photos on the wall to prove it—and one with Charlie next to his ancient fryer.

And now, the place is staffed with those who were pretty enough at fifteen to ruin the rest of their lives and work at Charlie's too, too long. So Jean doesn't mind that Jack goes there, but she won't step foot in the place. Which leaves you in the middle. Charlie's has a few trucks in the parking lot that are already inched up with snow, but no sign of Jack's. Inside, the straggly locals are somber and quiet and most have their backs to the dancers—no hooting and hollering tourists just off the river from a guided king-fishing trip. The Kenai is frozen. Sasha says Jack was here last night with Chako.

"I was hoping he was somehow still here," you say. And if not here, then you were hoping he was with Butch.

"I tried to make Chako leave without him," says Sasha. "That dumbass was making up his own shots again. I can't stand that shit."

"I hear you," you say.

"You want a drink?" she says.

"I've got another long drive ahead of me," you say. "No thanks to Chako the Chugger." From what you can tell, Chako and Jack have only two things in common—drinking and the navy.

"Jack in trouble?"

"He's never in it," you say. "He's just always next to it."

Something falls and lands on your shoulder, a lacy push-up bra.

"It wants to go home with you," says Billy, an older drunk and regular.

"Hell, I want to go home with you," says Billy's friend whose beard is twisted into three pointy dreads. Above the bar is a moose head with bugged-out gaga eyes and a tongue falling out of the side of its mouth. Bras hang from its antlers and there's a sign underneath the moose head that says, "Nice Rack." You're about to throw the bra back up on the antlers but stand on a bar stool instead. You lengthen the straps and tie each one around the base of the antlers so the cups cover the eyes, a push-up blinder.

"Darling," says Billy's friend. "He got a right to look. We all got a right."

"Darling," you say. "I fucking hate that moose."

There are worse things than death. Such as someone who keeps trying for it and failing. You wonder how many times you've risked your own life on patches of black ice to find Jack and drive him home to Jean. And each returning you tell yourself never again. But there's always a good reason. Jack is your brother and he protected you from a lot of shit growing up. Jack doesn't listen to anyone else but you. Jean is seven months pregnant. Then, Jean has three kids. Jean is taking night classes. This list is long and longer, an endless river, and it's easier to float than fight.

One of the longest nights was a Friday two summers ago, right before you met Hyde, when Chapter 576 of the Cornhole Association of America from Diddly Squat, Iowa—Sasha said they wore matching blue T-shirts—took over Good Time Charlie's. They were trying to dance on the stage with the strippers and Jack must have said something like, "Hey, farmboy shiteaters, what the fuck is cornhole?" and soon a bunch of corn-fed fists were swinging at Jack. Sasha called and said she and a bouncer had wrestled Jack away and she had locked herself and Jack in the office and then they both climbed out of the office window and were now down on Sterling Highway behind the Tesoro gas station in Jack's truck. You needed to come get him, he couldn't drive, and she needed to get back to Charlie's before the police came. You sped to the Tesoro, dropped off Sasha, took Jack to your place, and told Jean he was in a little brawl and was fine, and would be home in the morning.

You wetted a towel with warm water and handed it to him for his busted lip and somehow-not-broken nose.

"Just head shots," he said. "Don't worry. I'm still a beauty queen."

"You're going to scare your kids," you said.

"They need a little excitement." He yawned.

"You might have a concussion. You can't go to sleep."

"Where's your cribbage board?"

You pegged point after point and played round after round and didn't talk about what had just happened, how he could have been killed. One more punch. One broken bottle. A driving kick to the ribs. Instead, you bet ridiculous things for winning by five points and ten points and skunks and double skunks—the north pole, a Cessna airplane, a lifetime supply of king crab legs, a law that bans tourists from Alaska the month of July, three more hours of daylight during the winter, a cabin on the Kenai with its own boat launch—and then you slipped up and said, "You never having another drink."

He didn't look up from the cards he was shuffling and then he slammed the deck on the table like it was an empty shot glass. "You'd have to triple skunk me," he said. His black eye gleamed.

"Impossible," you said.

"Exactly."

"Well, then how about a tiny humpback I can keep in my bathtub?"

"Now *that*," he said, "I can do."

He told Jean how he had risked his life to keep the Cornholes from harassing the strippers. He had the whole town calling him a hero for a few weeks. There are breaks in the routine. Jack stopped drinking for a month after that night. He has intentions. He stopped drinking four months after his first kid was born. Three months after the second. Two months after the third. The phone calls stop but you wait for them—hear the ring of alarm when there is none. He is mostly a weekender, and by Friday you're on edge—on the edge of the edge. You drive by Charlie's just to make sure his truck isn't there. You're ashamed to admit that it is a relief when you do get the call, and after dropping him home you curl up into a deep and dreamless sleep. Then you cook an enormous breakfast of eggs and biscuits and tater hash and sheep sausage and eat almost enough to fill that hole in your stomach that says you're goddamned gutless.

How many drives in the middle of the night, in the middle of a blizzard or frozen shitstorm, until you've paid him back? Hyde says, "This has to stop, Gracie." Jean says, "This has to stop. I know better." "Stop" is one of those words that sounds like what it means. You don't know if it will.

One trip in July, you dragged Eagle Rock for kings in the combat zone, boats packed in the drift. A guide boat came too close and Jack said, "I only have room for one asshole in my life and that's my own, so get the fuck off me." Doormat and Hazmat, one boat over, laughed and Doormat said, "You sure you only got one?" You'd been on the river since three in the morning, the fog as thick as cigar smoke, your hands stinking of cured king eggs. Come on, sixty-pounder. Come on, you hawg, you hen, you motherfucking monster. Boats ahead had stood their nets up, the flag for a hooked fish.

"Get ready, Gracie," said Jack. "We're next."

You felt the hit and said, "Here we go," and cranked the rod back to set the hook.

"Goddamn, she set that bitch," said Hazmat.

"All for nothing," you said. There wasn't a lot of pull.

When kings run too soon, they're small and you don't want to waste a tag on one of them. They're not worth the meat, unless you're commercial. They can't spawn. A waste. Good for jack-shit, which might be why they're called jacks and you had one on your line.

"Another one of your bastard sons," said Hazmat to Jack.

"Poor little shit just wanted to get laid," he said back.

In the net, the fish that was pretending to be a king flicked and flailed. Jack held him against the side of the boat because if you brought him onboard you'd have to keep him. You leaned over with the pliers and worked on the hook that had gone through the black gums and out the side of the lip.

"I taught you how to set that hook," he said.

Because of his small size, the markings along the spine were inky and sharp, the exact shape of flared wings. "Look," you said. "He's got a flock of eagles on his back."

"Well, shit," said Jack. "He does. Now you really have to kiss him before you throw him back. That's super damn lucky."

This time you didn't argue. You aimed for the sleek slope of the cheek plate, right in front of the first gill slit—the high jaw—which is also your favorite part of a man. When you met Hyde, you liked him and tried to think why and then you thought, "He has the face of a fish," and you liked him even more.

Jack turned the net inside out to release him. "Who knows," he said. "Maybe now, after your nasty lips, he'll turn around and go back to the ocean."

"Fuck you," you said. But you hoped so. You still do. He'd live a little longer. Otherwise, what's the point of a fish with a flock of eagles on his back? Your mother has a similar hope. She lives in Chugiak and calls Jack every Sunday and he still won't talk to her, even after all these years. He always says, "There's no fucking way she can apologize for staying with our punchy old man, for what he did."

"But she tries," you say.

"You don't know what you're talking about," he says. "And that's because of me. I made goddamn sure he didn't lay a hand on you. Not her."

"You've told me some things," you say.

"And what? Now you're the expert?" he shouts.

And Jean will walk into the kitchen and say, "Shhh. The kids," and that's the end.

Chako doesn't live far from Good Time Charlie's. It's a walkable distance, more so if you're sober, but the problem is that Chako lives on an unmarked and unpaved offshoot that's a bitch to find, a bitch to drive. You've gone down the wrong thick-wooded road and had to wait a few miles for a wide enough clearing to turn around. You've been sure the truck would ram into the tall snowbanks on either side and you'd be stranded. You're sure this is going to happen this time. The road hasn't been plowed recently. And then you wonder how Chako and Jack haven't killed themselves driving these same roads after a blast at Charlie's which makes you think that miracles do happen, they just happen to the wrong people. Chako lives in an old trailer that doesn't have hook-ups, or a phone, of course it doesn't. He lives in boonie land. The trailer should have burned down long ago—he has a leaky old wood-burning stove and there is smoke worming its way out of a side window. No one knows why he hasn't built himself a little cabin. He's a handyman and he built himself a shrine of an outhouse. The outhouse is painted gold and has a golden onion-shaped dome on top so it looks like a Russian Orthodox church.

When it's warmer, you usually have the distinct pleasure of arriving when Chako is standing on his front steps taking a piss. He thinks this is hilarious. If you don't shield your eyes, he'll start shaking it around and making a show. You know this because once you decided to stare him down, shame him into zippering up. Big mistake. You told Jack, "He's so proud of his tiny dick it's a wonder he doesn't make a little golden onion to put on the end of it." At least you'd have something more interesting to look at.

"That," Jack said, "is the best idea you've ever had, Gracie."

No sign of Chako on the front steps in the middle of February. He probably pisses into a coffee can and tosses it outside. That's what you would do. You leave your truck running and climb the stoop and try the metal latch. It's locked, which is strange. It's never locked. Who would come all the way out here to ransack Chako's trailer? And for what? You bang on the door. No answer.

"I know you're in there," you yell. Chako's and Jack's rigs are parked on the side. "Get your drunk asses up."

The trailer doesn't shake with the weight of someone trying to stand.

"I'm going to break the door down," you say. "I don't have time for this shit." They're probably both passed out.

You shoulder the door and the old siding caves. Chako might as well have used a flap of cardboard for a door. You kick the rest of the way in. The smell of fire smoke rushes your face and you wave off the haze. You stop. That's not your brother lying dead on the floor with a red splotch of blood covering the chest of his gray shirt. That's not your brother's buck knife, the one he carries everywhere in a leather sheath on his belt, bloody and sharp and sitting atop an old newspaper next to three empty bottles of cheap vodka. You will not tell Jean that her husband died in his own vomit and that she has to raise three kids by herself. You will not tell your mother her son is gone. You will not bury him. That's not him. You back out of the kicked-in trailer and cover your eyes. You will go in again, and he will not be there, please God. The blood will not be there. The knife will not be there.

You count to ten. You step back into the trailer. There he is, on the floor, with empty orange juice cartons, bags full of garbage, fishing waders, old rusty thermoses.

"Gracie?"

"Jack?"

He moves his head. "Help me up," he says.

"Don't move. I'll go find someone. I'll call an ambulance."

"I'm fine." He props up on his elbow.

"You're not fine. Chako stabs you and you think you're fine?" You kneel next to him.

"He didn't stab me," says Jack. "Someone came and picked him up for a job."

"I thought you were dead." You look around for something clean to press to his wound.

"Well, I'm not," says Jack. "Not even close."

"Here." You grab the newspaper.

"Newspaper isn't going to do shit," he says. "The bleeding's stopped. Just hand me my jacket." He sits up and groans. You place his jacket on his shoulders.

"What do you mean the bleeding's stopped?" You can't believe the blade didn't cut a vein or artery or slice through his heart. Maybe it did. Maybe he's going to slump forward and bleed out any second.

"Vodka," says Jack. He uses you as a prop to stand. Then he looks around. There's a fourth bottle, half empty, and he grabs the neck. "For the drive to the hospital."

"Fine," you say. "And we should take this." You pick up the red-streaked knife and drop it into an empty cereal box. When you lose a piece of yourself, say a finger or a leg, you're supposed to bring it with you to the hospital. And for a while, the knife was a part of Jack.

You crutch him down the icy steps to the truck. Once the heat's blasting, the fumes of vodka, vomit, and fire smoke are sickening. You breathe out of your mouth. "You going to tell me what happened?"

"Wasn't planning on it," he says.

"Jesus, Jack."

"I believe his name was Jesus *Christ*."

"You tell me or you're walking," you say.

"You wouldn't make me walk." He looks out at the frozen trees. "But I'll tell you anyways." He takes a swig. Then swirls the bottle and takes another long drink.

"I'm listening."

"Gracie, Gracie. Always listening." He laughs.

"Goddamnit, Jack."

"You won't tell? Not even Jean? Not even that pussy boyfriend of yours? What's his name, Hicky, or some shit?"

You grit your teeth. "No one."

"All right. I did it."

"You did what?"

"I stabbed myself in the chest," he says. "I don't remember doing it, but I must have."

"That's it? That's all you have say?"

"I remember pulling the knife out," he says. "And thinking that would do me in. But then I woke up, figured I wasn't going anywhere—poured vodka on it all and drank some more."

"What about Jean and the kids?" you say. "What about me? You go apeshit on us all and you think it's a goddamn joke. I mean, I'm pretty sure I'm pregnant for god's sake. You're my brother. I can't do this without you."

"I hate to point out what's obvious," he says. "But you already did."

"You know what I fucking mean." You pound on the steering wheel.

He isn't fazed. "Does Hicky know?"

"His name is Hyde." You collect yourself, if there's anything to collect. "And maybe."

"Oh god," says Jack. "He's the kind of guy who knows when you're on the rag, isn't he? When will Gracie be bitchy? When won't she put out?"

"Sounds like you know a lot about it," you say.

"I'm right, aren't I?" he says.

"You're drunk." Which you somehow always forget when you're talking to him.

"I'm a lot more than that, Miss Slut."

"Watch it."

"Don't worry," he says. "You're going to be a terrible mother. The goddamn worst."

"I am," you say. "I really, really am." Because you can't even take care of your own brother, much less some helpless blob of a baby and when did you make the promise, "I will go down into the darkness with you," and when did you decide to keep it and your laughing sounds like you're crying, and your crying sounds like you're laughing. This is how you drive the snowy twelve miles to the hospital in Soldotna.

They admit Jack and you hand over the cereal box with the knife. You tell them how you found him and you have no idea what happened. They shrug and say, "It's February." You call Jean and tell her only that you're going to sober him up before you bring him home, which might be a while. You almost don't call Hyde, but when you hear his voice, you ask him to come to the hospital in Soldotna, that it's about Jack. The receptionist hands you a mug of coffee. In the lobby is a mannequin covered in fish hooks, articulating flesh flies, bright spinners and lures. You've heard the stories. Fishermen come in snagged and the doctor takes out the hooks and puts them on the same place on the mannequin. There's a line of papers taped on the wall next to her and the top one is titled, "Name the Manikin." You go down the list. Fish Hook Franny but then someone crossed out the *r*. The next two have definitions. Tina, my ex-wife. Marla, the fatass bitch sleeping with my husband. Then there's Fish Hook Hussy. Fish Hook Hawg. Fish Hook Fuck-Up. The Fish Hook Totem. The Lures of Eagle Rock. Dolly Varden Voodoo. Which is immediately followed with Vagina Voodoo. The Hook Keeper. The Fisherman's Curse. Fish Hook Whiskey. You try not to want the vodka Jack left in your truck. Fish Hook Hallelujah. Your favorite: WHAT I FUCKING FEEL LIKE RIGHT NOW scrawled in caps. Because they always find the most vulnerable parts—a treble hook at the base of the throat, ears and hands covered with tied flies. But the one that makes you cringe is the hook straight through the eye.

Jack probably won't remember this night, the hospital, your conversation on the way. You will. And if he does remember, he'll make a story out of it. "Some crazyasses broke in, looked like they rolled in moose turds, and tried to steal Chako's stove, can you believe it?

That stove was Chako's great-great-grandfather's. He hauled it on a snow sled across the tundra in 1875. I said, 'You're not taking this stove, you fucks. Have anything else. Have a bottle of vodka.' But they didn't want that. So one of the two starts acting real cagey, like he thinks he can take me. And I pull out my buck knife and say, 'You better think about what you're doing,' and I would have made a mess of him, if not for the slimy newspaper I slipped on in Chako's trashstash of a trailer and before I know it the guy is standing over me and I've been stabbed and then he spooks and runs off with the other guy and without thinking I pull that shit out." You'll be the nag of a sister who bitches him out on the way to the hospital. Chako will hear the story so many times he'll believe the stove is worth something, start telling his own stories about his wild great-great-grandfather.

The doctor comes out. You think, "He's dead. I shouldn't have moved him."

The doctor says, "Well, looks like he's out of the woods."

"Yes," you say. "Those damn woods."

They've determined the wound is self-inflicted by the angle of entry. The knife barely missed a vein, but all he needed was stitches. They're going to keep him overnight, do a psych evaluation when he's sober. You call Jean and tell her he's going to stay the night on your couch, a record bender this time. Chako was making up his own shots again and she says, "That goddamn Chako. I could kill him." Jack was supposed to do inventory at the auto-part store he co-owns with Doormat.

Hyde arrives with smoked salmon that was in your fridge and some crackers.

"There was an accident," you say. "He's OK. I can't tell you about it."

"But you will?"

"I will." You squeeze his hand. "Soon."

"Jean's not here?"

"Jean's not supposed to know."

"I think you should call her," he says.

"I think he should have to tell her."

"Is there anything you need to tell me?"

"Not now." You lean your head on his shoulder.

"You know what I do, while I wait for you?" he says. "I sew like my grandma."

You could go home, but you wouldn't sleep anyway. In the morning, they release Jack. Even they fell for his line of bull. Jack probably promised the guy a deal on a used transmission. The first thing he says when they wheel him out is, "Hicky, what are you doing here?"

Neither of you answer him.

"Chickenshits," Jack says. "You both thought I was gone, didn't you? And I bet *he* thinks you tell him everything, right, Gracie?"

You freeze.

Jack raises his eyebrows at you. "What, now you don't have anything to say?"

Two weeks later and you're at Fur Rondy. You still haven't had a phone call, not even from Jean just to talk. They're probably staying with your cousins in Anchorage. You and Hyde are staying with your mother in Chugiak since it's not too far away. You watch the blanket toss and go ice bowling and see the snow sculptures on Ship Creek. One of the first-place winners is called *Qasida*—Aleut for "go fish"—and shows an open-mouthed fisherman in a kayak struggling to catch a giant halibut that is right underneath him, fighting for its life, pulled up from the depths of the ocean. The fisherman has speared the halibut in the head and rides the wake. One more flip, one more thrash, and the kayak will capsize. Either one could win. You don't know if "go fish" is a command to the fisherman or a raised fist in support of the fisherman's demise.

For the Miners and Trappers Ball, you and Hyde dress up as lumberjack and lumberjill in matching red flannel shirts and work boots. You in the Carhartt miniskirt that Hyde made. You spot Jack and Jean on the dance floor, swaying to the slow music, their arms wrapped, their legs tangled. Her face is smashed into his shoulder. He has his chin tucked into her hair. If they could swallow each other under the streamers and glowing lights of blue, they would. But there's something about the way Hyde touches the arc of your back and keeps time with his fingertips—and you make up a stupid little song—*timber, timber, timber, you hold me just tight enough.*

BITE

❁

Polar Bear is in bed or she's tearing through the kitchen, eating and eating. Us kids find her scooping handfuls of flour into her mouth, the bag ripped open, white caked in the corners of her lips, white dust in her hair. She bites into raw potatoes, the earthworn skin and eyes, like they were apples. She sucks on woodchips she picks out from the bottom of the firebin, rolling them in her mouth until they are soft, her cheek bulging with the wet-splinter ball.

Polar Bear's stomach is big. She was sick and then she was better, and then she got sick again and Fox left to work on the slope.

"Maybe August," says Colleen. "Kitty won't be the youngest anymore."

Kitty is Fox's favorite. We know this and she knows this, but what she doesn't know is that we were all his favorite once.

Colleen finds Kitty's rag doll in a heap of shredded scraps.

"Look what she did," says Colleen. "It took me months to save up the fabric." And then Kitty rips pages out of one of Ben's books, *The Sea-Wolf*, the one he reads over and over, worn and cracked cover, broken spine he's glued.

"Why's she being such a shit?" says Ben.

"Don't say that," says Colleen.

"Shitty Kitty," says J.J.

"Stop," says Colleen. But she's itching to smile.

"Shitty Kitty," Ben spells with his hands for Rias.

And this is what we call her.

We fill up the tub with hot water and bathe oldest to youngest this time. When the water is gray and cold, it is Shitty Kitty's turn. But Shitty Kitty screams, claws at Colleen when she undresses her.

"She's running through the hall," says Colleen.

Ben grabs her. She hisses and scratches and he picks her up, her feet kicking. "Let's stop giving her baths," he says.

Polar Bear says this one is the worst. "This one is the last one," she says to her puffy feet. This flour-potato-woodchip blob of a baby coos and gurgles in her gut.

"Did you hear that?" whispers Colleen, out of range of Polar Bear.

J.J. nods. So does Ben.

Rias taps Ben's shoulder. What? he signs.

Ben rubs his belly. Polar Bear, he mouths, her belly is talking.

Shitty Kitty runs naked-fast away from us. We try to catch her, to force her flailing arms and legs into clothes and boots.

"Just let her be," says Polar Bear from bed. "I can't stand the goddamn screaming."

When Rias made Polar Bear sick-hungry, she had red spots on her face and then all over. Then she got better. "Didn't think nothing of it," she said. But she had been standing in the doorway of the homestead when Fox had shot a moose from the porch without so much as a warning, and Rias hadn't fussed or flinched. She knew something was wrong. "Take another shot," she said. And same thing, Rias calm like the gun hadn't gone off, and she drove back to Anchorage, she went to the doctor and he said that she'd had German measles. So Rias was born deaf.

Shitty Kitty crouches in the corner, and when J.J. walks by, she pounces and bites his leg, hard. He lets out a yowl and he's got his fist raised.

"No," says Colleen. "You can't do that."

"I'm about to knock her teeth out," says J.J.

"J.J., please," says Colleen. She puts a hand on his shoulder.

Shitty Kitty backs into the corner on all fours. Colleen reaches out to her and Shitty Kitty attacks, bites Colleen's hand and runs away.

"We have to do something," says Ben.

Rias nods.

"What the hell has gotten into her?" says J.J.

"I've just about had it," says Colleen. She shows the red marks of teeth in her skin, the blood.

Rias spells b-i-t-e h-e-r b-a-c-k.

There are never enough woodchips. Ben has to chop some up special for Polar Bear because the ones on the bottom of the firebin run out. Colleen keeps needle-nosed pliers on her at all times because Polar Bear yells when she's got a splinter in her mouth.

"Your turn," Colleen says and holds out the pliers to Ben.

"No, give them to J.J.," says Ben.

"She almost bit my hand off last time," says J.J. "Make Rias do it."

"I'll do it," says Colleen. "But we're all going in there."

"What the hell took you so long?" Polar Bear stretches out her cheek with her finger and we stand next to the bed. Colleen goes to it, but can't get a grip. The splinter is deep, a jimmy right in the side.

Polar Bear grabs the pliers from Colleen and holds them up. "You digging a hole?" says Polar Bear. "God."

"I see it," Colleen says. "That don't mean it wants to come out."

"Someone has to get this," says Polar Bear.

Ben takes the pliers and he feels around for the splinter. He has J.J. hold Polar Bear's mouth open.

"Stop," says Polar Bear. She jerks her head left.

Ben and J.J. jump back.

"It's no use," Ben says.

We have to wait for it to work itself back out.

"Scram," says Polar Bear. After we do, she calls out, "And get me a potato."

"Why aren't you talking anymore?" says Colleen, hands on her hips and looking down.

Shitty Kitty hisses from where she sits on the floor.

"We know you can talk," says Ben.

"Hiss."

"Shit. I don't mind if she never talks again," says J.J. "One less mouth going off around here."

"Rias here can't talk," says Colleen. "And you think if he could, he'd go around like you are?"

"Hiss. Hiss."

Polar Bear is a bellyache, a moan, a bucket filled and a bucket empty. Colleen and Ben stay home from school in turns to take care of her and then school ends and we all stay home. Polar Bear says she doesn't need us to ask Aunt Sheila to come and help. "What I need," she says, "is a little piece of quiet."

We tiptoe. We whisper. We stop talking out loud, mouth and spell with our hands like Rias, even J.J. who never learned to sign the alphabet when Rias first came back from school. Rias brings out his books. When he learned to lip-read, Polar Bear put them away and we all stopped learning to sign. Ben learned the most, and he still moves his hands whenever he speaks, a habit. The sign Rias uses for Fox is the letter *F* and Polar Bear is *PB*. Ben looks up the sign for *fox* and tries it, thumb and ring finger closed into a circle—the letter *F*, and then he puts the circle over his nose and twists.

"Looks like him," says Colleen.

For *bear*, Ben crosses his arms over his chest and flexes his fingers like claws.

"Let's do one for Shitty Kitty," says J.J.

Kitten is the letter *K* stroked on the cheek to draw a whisker.

"That's too nice for her," says Ben.

Rias pretends to bite his arm. We laugh.

"This is Polar Bear," says Colleen. She covers her mouth and heaves like she's sick.

"No this," says J.J. He grabs handfuls of air and stuffs his face, chews, and puffs out his cheeks.

We can't find Shitty Kitty. We look in cupboards, in the crawl space upstairs next to Colleen and Kitty's closetroom, under Polar Bear's bed where she's been sleeping tucked tight against the wall. Ben, Rias, and J.J. open drawers and check the top bunk in their room. We don't call out for her. We don't want Polar Bear to know. Outside is Fox's shed, what he used for a garage and where he keeps tools and parts for his truck. Ben has the key to the lock and he's the only one allowed in. We walk around it, slow, and there's a loose board, a spot of tunneled-out snow. Ben opens the lock and we go in and Shitty Kitty is nestled in a pile of old tarps. Nails and screws are scattered on the cement floor.

"If Fox sees this . . ." says Ben.

"Then we're all dead as fuck," says J.J.

"Stop talking like that," says Colleen.

Shitty Kitty opens her eyes, yawns and stretches out her arms, burrows her face into the pile of tarps.

"Let's hurry," says Ben. "I've got a bad feeling."

We let her be, pick up her mess and put the nails and screws back in the box on the shelf.

"Is that a truck?" Ben says, eyes scared open.

We all freeze.

"That's nothing," says Colleen. "Nothing at all."

We go back to work. Every axe, hammer, and scrap has its place and Fox notices when something's not where it's supposed to be. When he's home, he's in the shed working. Ben said he built it so it's warmer than the house, even in the middle of winter.

Colleen walks slow toward Shitty Kitty, kneels down.

"Don't," whispers Ben.

Colleen pets her black hair and Shitty Kitty sleeps, doesn't bite or hiss. Colleen cradles her head, picks her up, and takes her into the house. Rias refolds the tarp. J.J. hammers the loose board. Ben locks up the shed.

Shitty Kitty moves out from under the bed, and sleeps on the bottom corner of the mattress, near Polar Bear's feet. Each night, she inches up, sleeping at Polar Bear's ankles, her knees, her hip until she settles with her face nuzzled into Polar Bear's neck. This goes on for a while, but then Polar Bear yells for Colleen and we all go running up the stairs. Shitty Kitty is jumping on Polar Bear and Polar Bear, weak and pale and sweaty, is shielding her belly with one hand and swatting the air with the other. "Get her off of me," screams Polar Bear. We tackle Shitty Kitty, drag her to the closetroom, and close and sit against the door, her feet and fists thudding our backs.

"She tried to sleep on top of my stomach," says Polar Bear. "I told her no, she was too big, and then she went goddamn crazy. Don't let her in here anymore."

We hear the engine of Fox's truck arrive and cut off. He walks through the door and naked Shitty Kitty scrambles out from under the kitchen table and hugs his leg.

"Where the fucking hell are her clothes?" says Fox.

"She won't wear them," says Colleen.

We hear a choke-puke and Fox goes upstairs to see what's the matter with Polar Bear.

"You going to talk now that Fox is back?" says Colleen.

Shitty Kitty hisses and her eyes sliver mean. Rias is closest. She leaps and bites his calf. He grabs her, picks her up, and bites into the meat of her shoulder. Her scream breaks our keep-quiet-sign-and-whisper rule. Fox comes running down the stairs and Shitty Kitty crawls to him and whimpers.

"Rias. He bit me," she says.

"You fucking animals," Fox says. Before we can tell him why, he undoes his belt and flies at Rias, whipping-wild. We look away and brace for the slap of leather on skin, the floor.

Fox packs us up and drives us to the homestead so we're all out of Polar Bear's way for a few days. Shitty Kitty is wearing clothes again, because he told her to let Colleen dress her, and she's going on and on, talking Fox's ears off, like she's been saving up all her words for him while he's been gone—"and i go outside and there snow and leen say look and a moose there and i play in the snow...." We want to tell her to shut up, but we don't. She chit-chatters up a storm and Ben and J.J. roll their eyes and plug their ears. Rias rests his head on Colleen's shoulder.

We're done with our chores and chopping wood and Colleen says we should take a walk. Fox is snoozing. He dove into his stash of Jack-Slack as soon as he could. Shitty Kitty tries to follow us.

"No," says Colleen. "You stay here with Fox." She closes the door and locks Shitty Kitty in the homestead with the stopper latch on the outside.

The ground is a melting slush of white and brown and the trees drip down on us. We wander the woods above the swamp. When we make our way back, the door to the homestead is open. Only Fox could have opened it. Fox isn't there, but Kitty is, crumpled on the floor and crying. The smell of smoke lingers. The shirt on her back is shredded through. She's covered in red, swelling marks. Her bottom lip is bleeding down her chin. "Christ," says Colleen.

There's a pack of matches on the floor, a burned hole in one of Colleen's sweaters. The homestead Fox built by himself, log by log, and Kitty could have ruined it all with one spark. Kitty, Kitty, Kitty. We pick her up. We wipe the blood, clean her face. We shhhh Kitty. We hush.

SOME OTHER
ANIMAL

Ruby opens the pen and Sitka stands up on his hind legs, puts his paws on her shoulders as if to say listen, listen closely and she, not expecting this greeting, falls on her back. He hovers over her, licking her face, the warmth of his breathing a comfort, but anyone watching from a distance would think she was being mauled. She doesn't fight or flinch or shield herself with her gloved hands—she doesn't move. Sitka nudges her with his nose. Ruby stays still, the snow sinking beneath her. He growls and tugs on her blue scarf with his teeth until she chokes and hears the yarn tearing and she sits up. Then he releases her.

Mrs. Stern had stopped by to check on Ruby and said, "I got a job for you and you can't say no." For the next two weeks, Ruby would learn how to properly care for the dogs.

"I'll be right there," Mrs. Stern said, on the first day, when she answered Ruby's knock. "Let me get my boots." Ruby's mother, Kitty, had met Mrs. Stern at a poker game, a new night out after Ruby left for school. She said Mrs. Stern could drink all of them under the table, schnapps and more schnapps. "I liked her immediately," said Kitty. "She didn't act like a goddamn bridge player." Mrs. Stern walked down the steps in a black down-filled coat that went to her knees. Her hair, curly and brown with streaks of silver, frizzed underneath a wool hat with earflaps.

"I know," she said. "I look like a bag lady."

"Mrs. Stern," said Ruby. "Thank you for—"

"For the garage," said Mrs. Stern. She handed Ruby a key.

"Thanks," said Ruby.

"Please, call me Marsha," she said. "And thank *you*—we get to leave all this for a month." She waved her hand at the firs burdened by snow, the flakes falling to the ground. She jiggled the door to the garage. "Damn thing," she said. "Sometimes I give it a little kick."

Mrs. Stern headed toward the bags and cans of dog food, but Ruby was distracted. There were shelves and stacks everywhere—boxes of rice, macaroni, cereal, cookies; cans of peaches, corn, fruit cocktail, olives, soup; jars of pickles, mayonnaise; one tier dedicated to peanut butter. Four refrigerators hummed along one wall next to a free-standing freezer the size of a couch.

"I don't notice," said Mrs. Stern. "I forget. Ira. I call it his bunker. Something with the war. 'What?' I used to ask him. 'Where is this army we have to feed?' But I gave up. There are worse things he could do."

The malamutes eat twice a day, at ten in the morning, when the sun rises, and again at five in the evening—the sky settled in darkness. Ruby measures out the dog food in the garage. She's down to three cans of tomato soup, crackers, and a can of kidney beans at home, and she used the first check from Mrs. Stern to pay her utilities. She won't be paid again until the Sterns come back from their trip. The Sterns' garage is warmer than her mother's house—she has the thermometer set at fifty to save money. And her peanut butter has run out. She's eaten a spoonful at a time and she eyes Mr. Stern's jars. She could take one home, rearrange the rows, but she knows he'd notice. Every box and package and can is in meticulous order, rows and columns uniform, at attention.

Kitty died in June, right before solstice, during the night that wasn't night, the sun never going down. "I'm living two days for every one," she said. Kitty used the extra light as an excuse to tie more flies and paint beads, keep her focus from being sick. When she couldn't tie them herself, she gave Ruby instructions from her bed. Chuck, Ruby's father, had started the business under his last name, Silashouse. What the fishermen didn't know was that Kitty made half of them, and when Chuck left, she made all of them. Silashouse flesh flies were known for hooking rainbows in the murkiest rivers, the zonkers were known to get bites when most fishermen were skunked, and the beads—coral and swirled with glimmering ivory paint—were said to look exactly like salmon eggs. The Silashouse specialties, though, were voles and mice. Fashioned from deer hair and wire, their beady eyes glinted with startling conviction, and Kitty heard from Mr. Forne, the storeowner, that many were staged in pranks and practical jokes.

Kitty had made enough to live on, to be buried, and to let Ruby pay the bills for the past six months. Last week Mr. Forne called Ruby, said he'd sold everything and had one last check. "Why don't you take over Silashouse?" he said. "I'd help you." But she couldn't. All the supplies were shut away in Kitty's room.

Ruby framed her life: Twenty-two years old. Dead mother. No money. No other family in Anchorage—they all live in the lower 48 in places like Nashville and Omaha and she doesn't know them. And by the sound of those places, she doesn't want to know them. Nashville—gnashing of teeth. Omaha—oh my god. And she's in Anchorage—an old boat surrounded by ice.

Ruby braces for Sitka's weight, one hundred and fifty pounds of exuberant dog, and wraps her arms around him as much as she can. They sway for a few steps and when Ruby feels she might fall, she says, "Sitka. Down." She imagines him, in another life, as a music-footed dancer in a tuxedo.

Ruby has a routine: water, feed, sled, shovel, lock the gate. Some of the malamutes are show dogs, others were weight-pulling sled champions. They have sly, grinning expressions and plumed tails and thick, padded coats—white with charcoal coloring on their hoods and backs. Sitka, Mrs. Stern told her, turned out too large to be a show dog, but he is a natural at weight-pulling. She pointed at Orca, named for the black mask of fur on her face. "And this girl was too pretty to show. They can't have blue eyes. What a stupid rule."

"Mush," says Ruby. The four dogs—Sitka, Orca, Gersh, and Cosmo—lurch, and the sled moves forward. The Sterns have ten acres of woods and the dogs criss-cross a path through them at the slow, steady pace of stocky wrestlers, thick-boned and muscular. After about a mile, Ruby yells "gee" to turn right and head back. But the sled halts. The malamutes stand still with their ears perked up in black-tipped triangles.

She hears a rustling and turns. The man is wearing snowshoes and aims, eye on the scope of a rifle. He lowers the gun and puts a finger to his lip. "Shhh," he gestures. A stranger in the woods with a gun, a broad brown jacket and a rabbit fur hat. The man takes a few more steps, passes in front of Ruby and the dogs and kneels. He takes a shot and Ruby follows his line of sight to a moose, and from the size she guesses it's a bull that has already shed his antlers. The dogs start howling in long-winded coyote calls, Sitka an octave above the others.

The bull strides a short distance through the trees and collapses on its front legs, buckles to the ground face first, snow flying around him. He raises his head, struggles for footing, and falls again. Ruby holds onto the sled, ready if the barking dogs lunge and try to go after the wounded animal. Confident in his one shot, the man stands up. He approaches the sled with the rifle pointed at the snow, pats Orca on the head. The dogs, all at once, stop howling.

"Hey there, girl," he says to Orca. He looks up at Ruby, crinkles his eyes. "Well, you're not Mrs. Stern," he says. "She's an old battle-ax. I'd say you're more of a pocketknife." He smiles at Ruby through his dark, reddish beard. She doesn't smile back. The bull, a dark form through the trees, struggles halfway up and groans.

"So, pocketknife, do you have a name?"

"Fred," says Ruby. She puts her hand inside her jacket where she keeps a pistol.

"I doubt that," he says. "But what do I know? What do you do, Fred, when you're not sledding with dogs?"

There's a succession of grunts and huffs from the bull and the smell, not of blood, but the threat of blood.

"Aren't you going to take another shot?" says Ruby.

The bull falls again—felled branches snap.

"Don't need to."

"It's not moose hunting season," she says. But she would take a shot and end the bull's struggle if she had a bigger gun.

His name is Josef, he's a taxidermist, and he lives on property west of the Sterns'. He made a deal with them: any moose he tracks and shoots on their land, he gives them a fourth for the winter. Ruby thinks of the big freezer in the Sterns' garage, how it must be filled with years and years of moose meat. He has to walk back and drive his snowmachine and haul the bull home, gut him.

"After that, I'll bring some over for you," he says over the moans of the bull's slow death. "Then you'll be less likely to report me as a poacher."

"No," says Ruby.

"Don't tell me you don't eat moose."

"I do," says Ruby. And she wishes she hadn't said so.

Josef pats the dogs goodbye. "Couple of days," he says. "I'll stop by."

On the trail back, Ruby follows the plot: Woman meets stranger in the woods. Stranger kills woman. Or woman kills stranger. Or start again: woman meets stranger in the woods. Stranger lures woman with moose meat. Woman becomes strange. It never ends well.

The cupboards and pantry and fridge at her mother's house are almost empty. Ruby finds a can of tuna and eats from the tin with a fork and stamps her feet to keep warm. She quit school in Eugene, Oregon, to come help her mother—she chose the school because Eugene sounded like the name of a man who listened to jazz, wore cabbie hats, and kept butterscotch in his pockets—the opposite of Chuck, who she knew in pieces, shards her mother told her and the postcard he sent once. Ruby was seven and her mother went out to check the mail and, after flipping through the stack, handed her a glossy square of blue water, Niagara Falls. He'd written, "Kitty and Ruby, I got married. I thought you should know."

Kitty went back to the vise where she was tying flies. "That's that." She wound the whipping finisher around the hook. And then she stopped for a second and looked at Ruby. "Don't ever fall for a man who eats steak for breakfast." She turned and let out a nervous laugh and then she said, "That's fucking ridiculous," and buried her face in her hands.

All the fly-tying supplies, the hooks and fur, are shut away in her mother's bedroom. They came and took her mother's body and Ruby closed the bedroom door and hasn't opened it since.

Ruby locks the gate to the kennel with the padlock. She should get in the truck, her mother's green '79 Ford, and head home, but she unlocks the gate, steps inside the fencing and walks to Sitka's pen. He cocks his head to the side, questioning.

Sitka has to lie down to fit in the cab of the truck. Outside, the snow falls in lazy swirls, powder blunting the edges of everything, smoothing over the points of trees. For so long, Ruby has waited for a sharp stick, a sudden jab that will make her stop wearing her mother's slippers, their tattered flaps like slack mouths, and sitting on the bathroom counter, her feet in the sink, staring and looking for a trace of her mother in the mirror's reflection. Kitty had olive skin, hazel eyes, a smile wide and thin, and freckles dotting her high cheekbones. And Ruby, fair and blank, had checked her toes, her back, her legs for one marking, one freckle, and found nothing.

Sitka fills up the house. His presence and size overwhelm the spaces and rooms that Ruby alone has been occupying. He takes up most of her bed, his brow to her back, as if praying. Ruby listens to his breathing, a habit, waits for his light snore and the airy rhythms of sleep and when she's sure there isn't a hitch between breaths, she uncurls her fists from the pillow's corner and closes her eyes.

In the morning, she stands in front of Kitty's bedroom door, her hand on the cold metal knob. Maybe, with Sitka there, she will open it. "On five," she says to him. But her hand trembles and she stops counting at four. If she could open the door, she would gather up her mother's fly-tying wire and thread and feathers of blue, yellow and red, and dyed rabbit fur, and elk hair and deer hair and all the beads and tinsel and hooks, and she'd weave a shawl, bright and fringed, and go to the cemetery and dig up the coffin, wrap her mother's body and carry her into the woods where she should have been buried.

Ruby steps on the brake and the dogs slow down. Tracks and then a wide depression in the snow. Dark spots where blood must have been. The bull was shot here. The bull died here and was dragged off, butchered. The doctor. The butcher.

"I'm glad they're getting chopped off," Kitty had said, holding open her shirt and looking down at her chest. "Cross-eyed pieces of shit. I mean, look at them, Ruby."

"That's not funny, Mom."

"It is."

"No," Ruby said.

"If I say it's funny, then it is. Goddamnit, if we can't laugh I might as well croak." Kitty took her shirt off, stood in the living room topless.

"Mom."

Kitty shimmied. "Tell me they don't look cross-eyed."

Ruby bit her lip. "You're having surgery—"

"Fuck you," Kitty said. She reached for her shirt.

"Fuck you," said Ruby—quiet.

Kitty stopped buttoning and looked up. "Say it again. Like you mean it."

Ruby said it.

"Thank god." Kitty said. "We've got a little bit of normal back."

Every night Ruby says it will be the last, but she brings Sitka home with her. She and Sitka sleep face to face. "If you were a man," she tells him, "you'd smoke a pipe. You'd have a voice like gravel and honey and I'd make you read to me." She cups his jaw. "And you'd never wear flannel." Sometimes she wakes up in the middle of the night, panicked, because she doesn't know where she is, the darkness in the room spinning into phantoms of other places, convincing her she's back in Oregon, or that she heard her mother calling. Once, she wakes and pats the bed and when she feels fur she screams and jumps up—she forgot she'd been sleeping next to a dog. Sitka jumps up too, stands on the bed, and from across the room, he is a monster, a wolf creature. She flicks on the light. "We're sleeping with this on tonight," she says. But Sitka fidgets and tosses his head from side to side until she turns the light off.

Sitka stands in front of the open truck door, refusing to obey. "Come on, boy," she says. "Get in."

Sitka runs around the truck, and then bounds toward the kennel gate and stops in front of the lock. The other malamutes leap against the chain fence and yelp.

"Sitka, come here."

He ignores her and nuzzles the gate. Ruby walks toward him and he dodges and backs toward the woods.

"You're not funny," she says.

He pounces toward her and skids in the powder, and before she can reach, he leaps away.

She stands near the truck and points. "Let's go home."

He flings his head and throws off the wet snow and jaunts to the kennel gate.

Ruby drops to her knees. She pretends to stab herself in the chest. "Sitka, help, help. Oh my god, I'm dying." She falls as she had practiced for a theater class the last term at school before the phone call, her mother's voice unraveling, pleading.

Ruby waits and waits. He's testing her. She clenches her teeth against the cold and thinks of heavy things. A boulder. A mountain. A body filled with cement.

Sitka barks and the other malamutes join in, echoing his get-up, get-up yap. He runs at her and Ruby tenses as he jumps over her back, but she is stone.

He creeps up to investigate and sniffs her ear.

She snatches his collar. "Got you."

He's dragging her, snarling, and she's holding on and yelling, "Stop. Stop," and he does. A growl in his throat. Teeth bared.

"It's me," she says, not looking into his eyes. "Sitka, it's me."

His mouth softens.

Ruby takes Sitka to the house, and this night, shuts him out of her bedroom. He presses against the door and whimpers. She knows he won't sleep in the living room with the lamp turned on, but she won't sleep without the light cutting the darkness and slipping through the doorframe. And she knows she won't sleep with him so close. Fangs and teeth and wildness. His long-legged shadow stretches toward her, walks miles across her floor.

Orca and Sitka are pawing at the front of their pens so Ruby lets them out into the main run while she exercises the first sled. When she returns, the gate to the kennel is wide open—she forgot to lock it. Sitka and Orca are gone. "Whoa," says Ruby. The sled stops and she dismounts. Orca appears out of the trees and pads toward her, tail wagging.

"Sitka," she yells. "Sitka."

Ruby closes the gate and paces in front of the kennel. The snow is heavy, a blizzard is in the forecast that night and there are dog tracks all around from the sled. What she needs is a snowmachine and the Sterns don't have one. The nearest one would be at Josef's—hunter, poacher, neighbor. She unharnesses Candyrock, then Iditarod, Mitzy, and Chance. She locks the gate, pulls on the lock to make sure, and then drives down the long, winding driveway. Most malamutes, Mrs. Stern had said, given a chance to escape, will run and keep going and never turn back. "They'd make it to the Arctic if a bear or some other animal didn't get them first." Ruby turns right, west, and stops at three mailboxes, jumping out of the truck and brushing off the snow to read the names. The third mailbox reads Josef Emmit and then she notices the sign—J. Taxidermy. There are two buildings when she comes to the clearing, a small pine cabin with a porch and then a shop, open for business. The lights are on and she stomps the snow off her boots before going in.

The door jingles as it closes behind her. There are raccoons and bear heads, king salmon on the wall, the living dead in every corner. One moose stands, peering out the window, his magnificent rack sprouting like open palms from his head.

"Fred," says Josef. Ruby turns to face him and his gap-toothed smile melds into concern. "Everything all right?"

Ruby rides with Josef, her arms around his waist, trying not to hold too tight or be so close, but the frozen air stings her eyes. "These are my babies," Mrs. Stern had said. She ruffled Mitzy's ears. "Ira said no children, not in this crazy world. So I have my pups."

The snow hails down in a fury and they ride up the ridge, make a wide circle from the edge of his property into the Sterns'. They don't have much time before the sun sets, before the blizzard arrives, full force, a white-out. Ruby searches through the binoculars for a clump of black, a dog of a spot.

After an hour, Josef slows the snowmachine and points back to the direction of his place. He shouts over the engine. "We won't find him today." He reaches into his coat pocket and holds out a silver flask. Ruby declines and Josef takes a swig. The snow is thickening in the air.

The Sterns will be back in ten days. Ruby sees Mrs. Stern's eyes widen, taking in the news—as if Ruby had aimed a gun and shot her in the gut.

Josef parks the snowmachine. "You want a hot cup of coffee?"

Ruby has to get home. Her feet are numb, her hands, her face.

"Wait here," he says. He returns and hands her four packages of moose steak wrapped in white butcher paper. She isn't hungry, doesn't think she'll ever eat again, but takes them.

"I'll do a run everyday," says Josef. "I'll tell the neighbors to keep an eye out."

Ruby puts the white packages of meat in the freezer at her mother's house. She opens up every cupboard and scans the empty shelves for a hidden can or package of noodles. Then she moves a chair in, stands on it for a closer look at the bareness, the stray macaroni, the cracker crumbs, the dust of flour and spices. She should have borrowed the peanut butter. She paces the four corners of the kitchen, trying to ignore the animal noises coming from her gut, worry wrestling with hunger. "Stop it," she says to her stomach.

She sits on the couch, in front of the television, flipping through channels, hitting commercial after commercial of hamburgers and pies and dancing french fries and food, food, food. "You," she says to the television, "are a torture device," and clicks the off button. "You," she says to herself, "need to stop talking to appliances." At least when she brought Sitka home with her, she thought he understood what she was saying, at least she was talking to something that was alive.

She goes to bed, but after two hours, is still too hungry to sleep. She faces the freezer, grasps the handle. Sitka hit by a truck. "Mrs. Stern, I'm so sorry. I thought I locked the gate." Ruby drinks a glass of water instead. The nurse who had come into her mother's hospital room after the doctor gave his dooming verdict, a year at the most, had said the same thing, "I'm so sorry," and touched her hand. But it wasn't the nurse's fault. That Ruby felt obligated to respond to her and didn't know what to say made the sentiment cruel. There was another nurse, one with a ponytail of brown hair, who sat down next to Ruby in the hallway, and said nothing, and held her hand, traced a circle on her back. She stayed with Ruby until someone called her away. This one, her mother and Ruby called Nurse Nurse because "She's got that knowing way," her mother had said. "She's magic."

When Ruby approaches the kennel, the malamutes push their eager noses through the wire mesh. They know Sitka has escaped. They all stand on three feet of snow from the blizzard. She opens Timber's pen after shoveling the main run, and he rushes out and leaps at the caged dogs who start barking and rattling the fencing. She releases and harnesses the dogs to the sled one by one, first Timber and Cosmo as pair leads, Cosmo as a substitute for Sitka. Then she harnesses Chance, who snarls at both of them. "Hey," says Ruby, and she chokes up on his tug line. She switches Chance with Cosmo. Timber and Chance in the front. Orca and Cosmo are paired behind them. The four dogs charge the packed snow. Ruby scans the woods for movement, for tracks, for a sign. She leaves out three bowls of food along the sled route to entice Sitka back. She calls his name and her voice echoes, small and insignificant. At the top of a hill, the dogs start barking and running faster. Chance is leaning to the left to move closer to Timber. "Whoa," says Ruby. They don't listen. She hits the brake and the sled stops and she plants the snow hook. Timber springs onto his hind legs and Chance rises up to fight him. They twist their tug lines over the main line, which pulls at Cosmo and Orca, who start barking. "Stop it," says Ruby. She stands at Chance's back and reaches for his tug line to pull him away—she knows not to get between two fighting dogs. But then Chance falls backward and the force of one hundred and thirty pounds knocks her down and she lands on Cosmo. Cosmo, in self-defense, attacks and catches her arm, his sharp teeth ripping into her jacket. She tries to pull her arm away, but he clamps down. She buckles with the pain. She's shouting and flailing—she shields her face with her free hand and then he yelps and lets go. Orca has him by the back leg, and she's pulling him away from Ruby. He throws his head back, snapping the air in Orca's direction. Ruby scrambles to a safe distance. Four big, fighting, snarling, tangled dogs. Wolves in parkas, that's what they are. She checks her arm and there's a little bit of blood. The barking pitches into a frenzy. Ruby takes out the pistol and aims for the sky. She fires. The malamutes cower and look at her. Orca lets go of Cosmo's leg. Then Cosmo tenses up with a growl and Timber lunges in his harness toward Chance. Ruby shoots again. They settle, but now, in the distance, the dogs at the kennel are barking because of the gunshots.

A spot of Cosmo's fur on his hind leg is matted with blood. She approaches, kneeling. "There, boy," she says to Cosmo. "I'm just trying to help you." He's keeping his weight off his injured leg. She needs him to lie down in the basket in the front of the sled and have the other three dogs pull them back to the Sterns'.

Ruby sits near Cosmo and waits a moment. "I'm going to unclip your harness," she tells him. She holds out both hands in front of his eyes. "Please don't bite me again." He bares his teeth. She pulls her hands in. Woman shoots self and four dogs in the woods. Stupid dogs. Stupid life. "Let's try this again," she says. She moves slowly, presents her hands to him, and inches closer. "We're all going to keep calm. Orca is calm. Timber is calm. There, Cosmo," she says. She pets his ear. Her other hand smoothes over his head and shoulder to the harness. "Almost there." She holds the harness lead and coaches him to the basket. He whimpers as he limps. "We'll call the vet and get you fixed up," she says. Her arm starts to pulse and ache.

She leaves Cosmo on the sled and the other dogs in their harnesses and calls the vet. The assistant tells her to wash the bite on her arm with soap and hot water and bring the dog in. "No, you have to send someone here," Ruby says. She loses it on the phone, dissolves. "You don't understand," says Ruby. "I have no one." They make an exception.

The assistant, a short, thin woman named Sam, has known Mrs. Stern for ten years. Sam muzzles and then bandages Cosmo, says he won't need stitches. She inspects the punctures on Ruby's arm and then disinfects the bite and wraps it in gauze. "You're going to be fine," she says.

Ruby finds a crumpled box of saltines in the Sterns' garage and takes it home, her compromise for not stealing a jar of peanut butter, her consolation for being bitten by a dog. She devours one entire sleeve on the drive. In her mother's kitchen, she heats up water with a chicken bouillon cube found in a dark corner of a cabinet, and then fills a bowl with the broth and more saltines, smashing them as they soak. She takes a bite. "This is disgusting," she says, her upside-down reflection in the spoon mouthing the same words. She unwraps a package of moose steaks, runs water in the sink to defrost them apart, and cooks them on the stove. She sprinkles dried garlic and oregano. Sitka dead or cold or starving. "I know," she says. She takes a bite, burns her tongue. Sitka crumpled and broken, bleeding. "I know," she says again, chewing. The more she eats, the more she's crying. "What the hell is wrong with you?" her mother would say, is saying. And Ruby's mouth is hot, her throat, her hands. "Nothing's wrong with me," says Ruby. "What did you expect?"

"What did *you* expect," says the voice. And Ruby follows it to the door of her mother's bedroom.

"Tell me," says her mother.

Ruby throws opens the door and flicks the light. She attacks the table, empties a bin of elk hair and rabbit fur on the bed. Feathers and beads fly. She throws yarn and string and rips open pouches and unspools tinsel. She burrows in the nest she's made, covers her head with a pillow.

Her knee finds the first one. She didn't notice them before, but there are three small bumps underneath the sheet—two mice and a vole her mother made—she would have delighted at Ruby finally discovering them, her loud choke of a laugh shaking the mattress. Kitty gave a stash to Nurse Nurse who in the last months called with their adventures. "This one new hire was being a real bitch so I glued a mouse to a bedpan and you can guess what happened next.... I put one in the cotton ball canister and oh my Lord...."

Ruby holds the vole in her hand and cries.

Ruby doesn't take out the sled for two days. She's allowing her arm to recover is what she tells herself. When she's not with the dogs, she drives around, searching for Sitka. She doesn't sleep—her thoughts telling hunters to stop shooting, wolves to leave him alone, the woods to point him back to the kennel. Then, for the first time, Ruby decides not to feed them—one day won't matter. But then she thinks of Mrs. Stern. Ruby puts on her coat and snow pants over her flannel pajamas and trudges out to the green '79 Ford.

There's another truck already parked in the Sterns' driveway and Josef is propped against the kennel gate.

Before Ruby asks, he says, "No sign of him."

She wishes she could harness all the malamutes to the sled and have them pull her and the house and the kennel off the edge of a snowy cliff.

"Thought I'd check on the rest of the dogs," says Josef. He realizes what he's said. "Not that I thought—"

"I know," says Ruby.

He points at Cosmo's bandaged leg. "What happened there?"

She tells him the story as she opens the pens and collects the empty food bowls. Josef helps her carry them into the garage. He marvels at Mr. Sterns' collection, the bunker of food. And she's embarrassed, as if she's showing him a part of herself, the stored up things collecting dust and waiting to be opened, slashed, consumed.

"I wonder," he says. He moves toward one of the four refrigerators.

"Don't," says Ruby.

Josef opens the freezer door—a stock of ice cream. He chooses a carton, chocolate, lifts the lid. There isn't a spoon so he pats his pant leg and retrieves a pocketknife, scooping some into his mouth with the blade. Ruby leans her back against the counter, arms crossed, and he stands next to her, his shoulder almost touching hers. "You want some?" he asks. "It helps with dog bites."

"How about that flask?" says Ruby. He sticks the blade into the ice cream and hands her the whiskey. She takes a sip, concentrates on his face, the white scar that slashes his left eyebrow in half. "How old are you?"

"Old enough to be divorced and have a son." Because his voice cracks, because she's tired of winter and worrying and malamutes— she surprises herself and stretches up on her toes and kisses him. He backs away, startled. "Fred," he says. "You sure?"

She could say it was a mistake, she didn't know what she was thinking. Stranger gives woman moose meat. Woman kisses stranger. Or undresses him. "But not here," she says, as if the food-filled garage were a church, a sanctuary, hallowed ground. Woman and stranger naked in dog kennel. Dogs watch.

"Wait," he says. "You're just a kid." He sets down the carton and walks past her to the door. As he's closing it, he turns and says, "But you need anything—you let me know."

"Kid?" says Ruby to the jars and shelves around her. She carries the food bowls out to the kennel. The malamutes eat as if what is placed in front of them will be stolen, snatched away.

The next day, Ruby resumes the sledding schedule. She's locking the kennel gate and pauses. A muffled bark. Sitka? There it is again. Ruby races into the garage for Mrs. Stern's snowshoes. She walks out and the dogs rail against their pens, the metal ringing shrill and constant. "Sitka," she yells. She follows a track she plowed earlier on a sled run. In the half light, the branches darken against the backdrop of powder white. Above the treetops, the stars appear—iced winks clustering over the ridgeline. Another bark. "Sitka," she yells again. The kennel answers with a chorus of barking. Sitka is out there, miles ahead of her. Maybe she could drive to Josef's for the snowmachine. But that might scare him away. Maybe she could reach him, call him home. But the glittering snow and her throbbing hands tell her the temperature is dropping. Woman freezes to death in the woods. Bears eat frozen woman. Or wolves. The malamutes are howling now and she hears Sitka, his sharp cry rising above their long, lonesome bay, and she knows that this is as far as she can go—and she waits, before turning around, for all of them to stop wailing at the moon that isn't there.

MR. FUR FACE
NEEDS A GIRLFRIEND

Eddie thinks Spook is still alive and so do I. She can't be dead. People like her never die, they drink Jippers and smoke Big-Z cigars every day and they outlive all the Quiet Marys of the world. She'd say to me, "Listen, Puppygal, you're good enough for the both of us. I'm going straight up to that heave-ho in the sky just for knowing you."

Ma is the one who made Mutts hire Spook. Captain Mutts, that's my dad, who I call Mutts and Ma calls Captain Mutts, though she's the one who drives our boat, the *Halibut Hellion*, and she's the one with the fish sense and the one who keeps everyone from killing each other. This woman showed up at the Seward dock with her homemade knives and waited for a cleaning station and none of the bibs would let her in. I told her she could have my space when I was done, but Ma came to the dock. The bibs were all talking about the woman, said she was so ugly she'd make a boat spook, jump water, and travel by land, which is how she got the name Spook, and it stuck and Spook didn't seem to mind. Ma told them all to stop being dicklicks and to clear a space, she needed another fish cleaner. They stood looking at her and not moving until she gave Yo-Yo the slap-eye and he hustled to spray off his board. We already had Eddie to clean fish with me, who the bibs call Fast Eddie because he isn't so fast, if you know what I mean. At first, Spook wasn't so fast either. I'd watch her with her wiry silver hair in a messy ball on the top of her head and her slow, small old hands—they were more wrinkled than the rest of her. But her knives, I'd never seen ones that made these bitchass black bass slay like butter. I wasn't the only one who noticed. All the bibs were crowding around, wanting her knives. Spook winked at me, "Puppygal and Eddie are the only ones who will be getting these and then we'll see," she said. The next day, she gave me and Eddie three knives each, grooved moose and caribou antler handles, and the blades she said were a secret, but I know she used old bandsaw blades. When I told Ma, she didn't believe me. "Shit if I've ever heard it," Ma said. She says this a lot, and most of the time to my uncle Dude and uncle TooSoon, who are both Mutts' brothers. But when Ma saw the knives in action she said, "Those beat the hell out of those Nox knives everyone uses, now don't they?" loud enough for the whole dock of bibs to hear.

From then on, Spook, me, and Eddie owned the station. You give us a gnarly-mouthed ling or a chicken flounder or butt and we are filleting fools. And when some cruiser tourist comes up and asks Spook if the halibut she's cutting is a salmon, we get to laugh at that shit because we're not going to lose tips, we're turning charters away, we're in hell-high demand up to our gut-splattered elbows. We always cleaned all the fish for the *Halibut Hellion* and Uncle Dude and Uncle TooSoon's boat called *R U UP?* which was a joke because you never knew which one of them was sober and which one was blazed, but they take turns, and then it got a whole new meaning on a boat when the waves are cobbing and you've got a ticket on board who you told to take bonnie pills but he said, I don't get sick, and next thing you know, you've got a dumbass Texan who thought he was a toughblood because he'd been tuna fishing a few times in Cabo and of course he's bellyflat, chumming the water and wailing for his mama's mama.

But now it's back to me and Eddie, and Spook is gone. I catch Eddie staring at the water, ghost-faced and forgetting that he's supposed to be hacking fish and I know he's thinking about her. Not too many people are nice to Eddie, and if you are, you can't get rid of him. He's yours, forever. He'd cut off his hand if you needed him to and when the Coast Guard found him and the stolen boat, he was screaming for Spook and he tried to jump back into the water right after they pulled him out. He almost died of hypothermia. Uncle Dude and Uncle TooSoon and me didn't leave his side until he promised he'd stop throwing himself in and then, for two weeks, I had a rope around his leg tied to mine while we were working just to make sure he wouldn't bail.

We're swamped with silvers from the salmon derby and I can't do it all by myself. "Come on," I tell him. "Let's turn these out so we can go get sourdough pancakes," which are Eddie's favorite, and Tanna at the bakery keeps a bottle of her special blueberry syrup stowed away just for him.

"And a simmerin' roll," he says and picks up a silver by the gills.

"Two simmerin' rolls," I say.

We slog through two carts of silvers and then Uncle TooSoon tells me there's another load that needs to be picked up.

"No," says Eddie. "No. No. No."

"It's the last one," says Uncle TooSoon. "You and Puppygal can handle them."

I still wince at the nickname that Spook gave me. I've always been Pups and she added the "gal." There's no way to change it now.

"Aye Aye, Mr. Fur Face," I say, throwing out what Spook called him.

"Don't give me those ugly looks," he says. "Or I'll start calling you Puppy Chow."

"At least you can see my face," I say. His is mostly covered in a bushbeard—he and Uncle Dude have a contest every year for who can grow the longest and scariest hair and they get drunk and shave it after the first moosekill of hunting season.

"It's a good thing *you* can see *my* face," says Yo-Yo from his station. All the bibs laugh.

"I feel sorry for Fast Eddie here," says Uncle TooSoon. "Having to deal with you two lovebums."

"Vomit and more vomit," I say.

"Yo-Yo, he smells," says Eddie. He plugs his nose.

"Shit, man, you got me there," says Yo-Yo.

When Spook met Uncle Dude and Uncle TooSoon, she said, "Mr. and Mr. Fur Face need a girlfriend. Hell, the whole state of Alaska needs a girlfriend."

"They can't keep them for more than a month," I said. I told her they even once shared a girlfriend, her name was Karla, and she couldn't tell them apart, being born in the same year so they say they're Irish twins even though they aren't Irish and then with their matching beards, and it's not like anyone could blame her, though, after she left, Ma said Uncle Dude and Uncle TooSoon should just marry each other, roll all the trashy family goings-on into one big blast. Uncle Dude was born in January and Uncle TooSoon was born in December, two and a half months early. Mutts said he wasn't supposed to live. But he did and Mutts said that ever since, they've both been worthless knuckleheads.

"They could be worse," said Spook. "Believe me, I know."

One day, Eddie took another break to go to the bakery for a second round of sourdough pancakes. "Where?" he said, when he returned, and pointed at his station. His knives were missing.

I patted his coat pocket. "Did you take them with you?"

"Give 'em back," he screamed.

The bibs stared at him.

"You fuckers," I said. "Who took Eddie's knives?"

"How much they worth to you?" said Yo-Yo.

"I still have a knife," I said. "And I will kill you."

"Kill. You," said Eddie. He paced around the stations with his sleeve between his teeth.

"Tell us where they are," said Spook. "And I'll sell you your own knives."

"Where'd you put them, Tin?" said Yo-Yo.

"Someplace cold," said Tin.

"Tell us where they are *now*," said Spook.

"IPCO's freezer," said Tin.

I ran off the dock toward the main. Yo-Yo followed me.

"Go away," I said.

"You wouldn't kill me," he said. "You like me too much."

"Go screw yourself," I said.

"I will." He smiled. "And I'll think of you."

"You piece of shit, you don't understand anything." Now every time Eddie went on break he'd have to take his knives with him, and he'd check and double-check and triple-check. Eddie didn't bounce back the way most others do. The smallest things were mountains to him.

"We didn't know he'd go bonkers crazy," said Yo-Yo.

"Yes you did," I said. "And you did it anyways."

Eddie didn't fillet any more fish that day. He sat on a gill bucket with his knives splayed on a towel in his lap, cleaning and rubbing and inspecting them.

"See that," he'd say to anyone who passed by. "That's me. Mine." Spook had engraved our knives—mine with "Pups" and his with "Ed."

Spook sold knives to the bibs. She charged them double. "Asshole tax," she said. They looked exactly like mine and Eddie's, but the bibs noticed something was wrong after a few days.

"These aren't sharp," said Yo-Yo. He'd made a shit pile out of a perfectly good yellow eye.

"These knives, they be rigged," said Tin.

"You just don't know how to use them," said Spook. To prove her point she demonstrated with their knives, sliced and filleted in long, clean, gliding strokes. I'd seen her use the same movement every morning when she stretched and faced the ocean before a shift, rocked back and forth, and then carved the air with her tai chi routine. "Your knife is only as dull as you are," she said.

Tin and Yo-Yo both looked at Eddie who was swording through a ling cod with ease.

Yo-Yo puffed up, about to say something. "And Fast Eddie—"

"You better shut your mouths right now," I said.

"I've got a sharp knife here," said Yo-Yo and he grabbed his crotch. The bibs choked on their laughter.

Spook pointed at Yo-Yo with her blade. "You ever do that again and I'm cutting what little you have right off, you hear me. I'm too old for your shit."

Yo-Yo and Tin backed away with their hands in the air.

"We surrender," said Tin.

"Lady, I was just playing," said Yo-Yo.

"Shake," said Eddie. "Handshake."

"Not today," said Spook. "Look where his hand has been."

Uncle Dude walked up with a cart. "What's with the standoff?" he said to Tin and Yo-Yo. "Spook got a gun?"

Spook tapped her temple. "Oh, I'm packing heat," she said.

"I need to get me some of that," he said and slabbed a few chicken halibut on my station. "We got skunked today. Even used Pups's ma's famous mack and cheese bait bomb and got no dough. Got shit dog sharks and shit skates and chickenshit halibut."

"Shit fish for a shit captain," I said.

"Ohhh," howled Yo-Yo and Tin in unison.

"You better figure out why Ma's mad at you again," I said. "Or you're never going to catch a decent fish."

"I think someone ate bananas on our boat," he said.

When someone books a trip, we tell them no bananas. Don't eat them for at least a day before you fish. Not even banana bread. Don't touch them, don't smell them. Mutts had someone make big "no bananas" stickers for the *Halibut Hellion* and the *R U UP?* They look like no smoking signs, except there's a bunch of bananas circled in red. Bananas are bad luck—they keep the fish away.

Ma's the one who can track the tides and find the pockets, and if she's not talking to Uncle Dude and Uncle TooSoon on the water, they're not going to catch fish. Everyone knows Ma's record. Everyone knows she's the best. Ma's been trying to beat her own barndoor halibut record for as long as I can remember. Her name and the date and the measurements and weight are etched into a post at the weigh station on the dock. She caught a five-hundred-pounder near Montague Island and then decided that if she could do that, she might as well marry Mutts. That's what she says. When she's sore at Mutts, for, say, loaning money again to Uncle Dude and Uncle TooSoon, she'll let him know by saying, "I didn't reckon my five-hundred-pounder would get me a flounder." And he'll say, "What the hell is that supposed to mean?" and she'll say, "You know what that means." And he'll say, "Am I the flounder? Is that right? I'm the flounder?" and he starts flailing and stomping around in a crazy swimming dance, circling the coffee table until she gives in and casts an imaginary fishing line and reels him in. He moves closer and closer to her and tilts her back and kisses her neck until she laughs. He'll say, "I bank my life on that laugh. You see, Pups."

But this summer, the summer after Spook, Mutts's dancing hasn't fixed anything and Ma hasn't spoken to him or Uncle Dude or Uncle TooSoon for three days. If it weren't for the salmon derby, Uncle Dude and Uncle TooSoon wouldn't have any fish at all aboard the *R U UP?*—anyone can catch silvers. I finally get the story from Uncle Dude and Uncle TooSoon after they've had four too many Jippers at their trailer. They'd been playing poker at a shady bar called Salt Lickers up near Primrose Lake.

"Some bad shit went down," says Uncle Dude.

"One guy got stabbed," says Uncle TooSoon.

"She doesn't need to know *that*," says Uncle Dude. "This one jackass thought we were hustling and then it went down the shithill." He tells me that Mutts had lent them money so no one would be after them, which was nothing new, except that he had to dip into my college fund which I didn't even know about. "Your Ma started it when you were born or something," Uncle Dude says. "It's all her own money. She said, 'Pups is getting out of here. Pups is going to college. Pups is Pups and Pups this and Pups that.'"

"Shit, we didn't know it was from your college fund," says Uncle TooSoon, "or we wouldn't have taken it."

"Liar," says Uncle Dude. "We would have still taken it." He tips his can toward me. "No offense, Puppygal. You know we're sonsofbitches."

"Sonsofbitches from the get-go," says Uncle TooSoon.

"No, what did she call us?" says Uncle Dude. "Sacks of shit-for-brains, that's what it was."

"And something else," says Uncle TooSoon. "What?"

"It must have been lucky scum," says Uncle Dude.

"Leeches," I say. But they don't hear me.

"Here's to the best uncles in the world," says Uncle TooSoon. He raises his beer and then chugs it down.

"Chin up, Pups," says Uncle Dude. "She'll come around. She always does."

But Ma starts to sleep overnight on the *Halibut Hellion* and I wish Spook was here so I could ask her what to do.

Spook knew how to handle everything. Last Summer, Eddie and I were learning how to run. I wanted to join Ma in the Mount Marathon— she runs every year wearing a Viking helmet with her friend Trish from Anchorage, who wears an American flag as a cape. One and a half miles up the mountain, and one and a half miles down, and most runners cross the finish line covered in dust and mud. Then there are the bleeders who fall on the rocks and the sliders who go butt first down the steep trail at the very top. Every year I say I am going to run with Ma, who will flex her calf muscle and say, "That's where all my cleavage went," and last year I actually tried to train for the race. Eddie would walk behind me until he'd had enough, and then he'd sit and wait. We started with flatter trails in the woods near the salmon spawn because it wasn't too far from the docks. I'd wear shorts under my pants and take the pants off when no one could see. Sometimes Spook would come with us to look for wild mushrooms. She had spent some time in Fairbanks hunting for morels for local chefs the summer after a big wildfire.

"Fire and rain and what you get are gourmet shrooms," she said.

She'd smoke a Big-Z cigar and talk about all the jobs she'd ever had, the oyster farm in Homer, tagging Dall sheep, running sled dogs for Iditarod trials.

"I'm old and I'm tired," she said. "As soon as I sell enough knives, I'm retiring. I'm going to buy me a little cabin and do whatever the hell I want."

She promised Eddie she would teach us how to make the knives. "But not today," she said. "Some other time."

Once, Eddie walked up to us with dirt around his mouth and dirt in his hand. He was smiling. "I found," he said, and he opened his palm and showed us the brown mushrooms.

"Those are poisonous," said Spook. "I told you."

"Oh my god," I said, looking at the dirt on his mouth. "He ate them. Eddie, did you eat these?"

He nodded. "They were good."

"I told him," said Spook. "Didn't you see me tell him they were poisonous and not to touch them?"

"We're dead," I said. "Holy shit. We're dead."

"We are not," said Spook. "Go call an ambulance."

I ran to the nearest place with a phone, Safeway, where Eddie's dad, Mr. Dean, was the manager. I was supposed to take care of him and now he could die. Ma said that we were all given things to take care of, to be responsible for. She had the *Halibut Hellion* and the *R U UP?* and I had Eddie.

Mr. Dean called 911. "They said the fire station's the closest to us," he said.

Spook, dragging Eddie, followed me, but at a much slower pace. They arrived right before the firefighter emergency van came, sirens busting up the calm, foggy afternoon, and all the shoppers in the parking lot stopped and stared. The firemen rushed out with a gurney and Spook gave them the mushrooms.

"Get me the charcoal," said the biggest firefighter. "Hey buddy, did you eat these?" he said.

"No," said Eddie, flapping his arms. "No. Those are bad."

The firefighter looked at Spook and me. "Did you see him eat them? How long since he ate them?"

We hadn't seen him eat them. We guessed fifteen minutes.

The other firefighter had Eddie sit on the gurney.

Eddie let out a high-pitched gaggle of laughter. "I joke," he said. "I got you. All you. I got you. Me. Mud here," and he paintbrushed his fingers down his face.

The bigger firefighter turned to Mr. Dean. "Even if he is joking, we have to assume he ate them, just in case. Protocol." He strapped Eddie down to the gurney and then sat him upright. He held up a red plastic bottle with a straw. "Buddy, you need to drink this so you can get better."

"No," said Eddie. He fought the straps. "I joke. No."

"Last chance," said the firefighter, to Mr. Dean. "Or I have to put a tube down his throat."

"Come on, Eddie," said Mr. Dean.

"It's like a mud milkshake," said the firefighter. "Who do you know that's ever gotten to drink a mud milkshake?"

"Not me," said Spook. "Not Puppygal."

"OK," said Eddie. He sipped on the straw and then smiled, black grit covering his teeth.

"There you go," said Mr. Dean. "You drink that whole thing and you can have all the real milkshakes you want when this is over."

The firefighters wheeled the gurney into the van and Mr. Dean went and sat in the passenger seat. The siren lights whirled.

And then Tin and Yo-Yo walked up to the curb. Yo-Yo whistled at me. "You've got legs," he said. "Who would've thought?"

I was still wearing my shorts. I'd forgotten my pants in the woods in all the excitement over the poisonous mushrooms. "Eddie's in an ambulance and you're whistling at me?" I said. "I should punch your face in."

"Fast Eddie's a trooper," Yo-Yo said. He tilted his head toward me. "She's kind of cute when she's mad."

I lunged and Spook caught me. "That's enough," she said.

They were laughing.

"You boys better go back to the docks," she said.

I turned away so they wouldn't see I was crying. Spook and I walked back to the woods. "Eddie's going to be all right," she said.

"I know," I said.

"I'm not going to say they like you and that's why they're mean," she said. "But they might. Too many people go and get confused and mistake real meanness for like, and even love. They aren't that kind of mean, not yet anyways."

"Well, I hate them."

"You might change your mind someday. But remember this one thing." She stopped walking and stood in front of me. "You're nobody's girlfriend. You're better than that."

I didn't know what Spook meant exactly, but I figured it was similar to Ma saying some people were deckhands, and some were captains, and she sure as hell wasn't raising me to be a deckhand. She also said that I wasn't better than anyone else or special because I was Eddie's friend. He wasn't a medal I could wear around my neck.

Turned out, Eddie hadn't eaten the mushrooms after all. Mr. Dean brought him to the docks after two days. "The funnyman's back," he announced. "A real jokester."

The bibs gathered around Eddie and high-fived him.

"I'll do better," I whispered to Mr. Dean.

"You do fine," he whispered back. "But whatever you do, don't mention milkshakes to him."

Ma's been sleeping on the *Halibut Hellion* instead of coming home. Mutts is sitting at the kitchen table, smoking, even though he's not supposed to smoke in the house. But I don't remind him. I sit down.

"Uncle Dude and Uncle TooSoon told me," I say.

"They weren't supposed to," he says. "No one was."

"I don't even know if I want to go to college."

He winces. "This one's on me, Pups. I'm supposed to be the one to give up things. I have to fix it, not you."

I lay my head on his shoulder. "You will," I say.

He kisses the top of my head. "Go check on your ma," he says. He hands me a twenty. "Take her a smoked pastrami and a jalapeño brownie from the Smokestack. Get yourself one too."

The Smokestack is Ma's favorite place to eat. The owners took four old Alaska Railroad cars and made them into a diner. They smoke all the meat and Ma says there's nothing better, she'd make them smoke Mutts if she could, just so she could have that hickory smell around all the time.

When I yell for Ma at the harbor, and she climbs down the *Halibut Hellion* and sees the food, she says, "He's feeling guilty. He should."

We sit in lawn chairs on the deck of the *Hellion*. She sips a mug of red wine. "Me and God have been having some good talks about assholes," she says. She laughs. "About assholes in the world."

"I know what happened," I say.

"Of course," she says. "Those shitfaces couldn't even do that— keep their fat mouths shut." She takes a big bite of pastrami. "It's going to take a lot more than this to make things right."

"How come you never told me?" I ask.

"It's a lot of pressure," she says. "I was waiting for when you were older, when you knew what you might do with your life. And maybe you don't use it for college. But what if you wanted to go to flight school, or take a trip and get the hell out of here, or things I never—" She raises her mug. "I'll be damned if they take that away from you."

"Or my own boat," I say. Me and Eddie already have a name picked out, the *Atta Girl*.

She hesitates. "Or that too," she says. "As long as that's what you really want." She unwraps the brownies. "Chocolate and jalapeños, who would have thought they'd be so good."

"You're coming back, right?"

"I've figured out what to do," she says. "Going to sleep on it and make sure. Tell those boys and Mutts to meet us here at five in the morning. Then you and I are going fishing."

I stand and start to leave. "But you're coming back?"

"Five sharp," she says.

We'll never know what really happened the day that Spook disappeared. We were all at the weigh station dock, waiting for July 3rd to become July 4th and for the midnight sun to darken so we could watch the fireworks. That's when she probably scoped out which boat to take. I didn't even know she knew how to captain a boat. When Ma would offer to take her fishing, she'd say, "I don't do water. Not after working on an oyster farm."

Later, after waking up early and having breakfast, Ma and I, in matching red, white, and blue face paint, were heading to the lineup for the Mount Marathon. She had on her Viking helmet and people we knew would slap the top of it as they passed her and wish her good luck. That's when Mutts caught us and told us that Eddie was missing and that the Coast Guard was investigating a stolen boat in the bay. "There's someone in the water," he said. We ran to the docks and huddled around Mr. Dean. He and Eddie had been having sourdough pancakes at the bakery and it was crowded with tourists, line out the door, and he went to use the restroom out back, he had to wait a while, a woman with four kids was holding everyone up. Then when he returned, Eddie was gone. Someone had seen him go out the door, but that's all the information he had. Too many strangers and visitors, too much busyness. What we think happened is that Eddie spotted Spook and followed her to the sailboat, and he snuck aboard, or she let him come along. But that doesn't sound like her, letting him on the boat only to jump ship and leave him alone in the middle of Resurrection Bay. Or maybe she planned to go farther out and land on Fox Island and, again, Eddie made her change her mind. We know she was in the water because Eddie jumped in after her. He kept calling for her, the Coast Guard said. But he won't talk about that day, he won't say anything.

A week after her disappearance, some man came asking about her at the docks. He walked like a kicked dog and he wanted to know about antler knives that had been stolen from him—drove in from Homer.

"Those ones you're using look like ones I made," he said.

"Mister," I said. "I think you're mistaken." I didn't know why I wanted to give this sad man a hard time.

"The thing is, those are my knives," Mister said.

"These shitty things?" I said. Spook was gone, Eddie was still recovering, and I didn't really care if he looked like he'd had his guts punched out, I was not going to give him my knives. Stolen or not. But I should have had Mutts or Uncle Dude or Uncle TooSoon there to back me up before I said anything like that.

"What she means is," said Yo-Yo, "how much for you to get the hell out of here?"

We paid Mister seventy-five for each antler knife at the station. I was thinking about dropping my money in a slick of fish slime and blood before I gave it to him, but I saw him tearing up. No one told him about Eddie's knives, which were safe with him at home where he was resting after being in the hospital. Mister leaned over the wooden rail of the dock and looked out at the ocean. He turned and said, "Two years and I thought I knew her. She took my knives. She took everything." He put his hand over his mouth and shook his head, back and forth. He left after an hour or so. They never found Spook's body, or a campsite, or any trace that she might have somehow swum to shore in the cold water and lived. I think she made it, however impossible it is. An emergency wet suit was missing from the boat. And there are so many coves and old army outposts and places where she could be hiding. She could be sitting next to Godwin Glacier up in the peaks right now, sucking on glacier ice. But if there's one thing that Eddie hates the most, it's being left behind. Not being allowed to go with you. I don't understand how Spook could leave us all without a warning. Easier for her to leave, I guess. But not easy for me or Eddie, or even for the stranger from Homer.

The fog is thin, and even at five in the morning, I can tell the roll will burn off into a clear and sunny day. Uncle Dude and Uncle TooSoon and Mutts and I are waiting for Ma. She walks up behind us carrying a box of bait. Mutts tries to help her and she waves him off and sets the bait down on the dock. "Now," she says, "what to do with a bunch of good-for-nothings."

"We're sorry," says Uncle Dude.

"You know what's really sorry?" she says. She points at each one of them. "You, you." She stops at Mutts. "And especially you."

Mutts raises his hands to speak.

"You all shut up and listen," she says. "This is how it's going to be. Each of you is going to replace the full amount that was taken. Each of you. Which means you're tripling it. I'm giving you three years. You get a good tip—it goes into Pups's fund. You got money for beer—it goes into the fund. You find a quarter on the ground—it goes into the fund. You'll do without. You'll roll your own damn cigarettes. You'll take extra side jobs hauling shit. Whatever you have to do. And if, after three years, you don't have enough, I'm selling the *R U UP?* so there is enough. And you'll go back on the slime line, you understand?"

"Yes," say Uncle Dude and Uncle TooSoon.

Mutts says, "But what about—"

"I don't know about you and me yet," she says. "But Pups and I are going fishing."

Ma has me drive once she thinks the Coast Guard won't be watching. Three hours later, we're heading east out of Resurrection Bay toward Montague Island. Then she drives and I jig for ling cod out the back, hook one after the third bounce off the bottom. Lings are the ugliest fish I have ever seen, bloated lizard bodies with spiky fins and huge mouths, but they put up a good fight. Halibut are a pain to catch—even a chicken feels like a thousand pounds you have to peel off the bottom—and then, after all that shoulder-breaking reeling, you throw it back. I limit out with two keepers and Ma has me catch two more for her. In the holding box, the lings flop and slam against the sides.

"Time for mack and cheese," Ma says. I fill a brown bag with chopped mackerel and squeeze bait sauce over them. I tie off the bait bomb bag with the end of the fishing line on a salmon rod and cast out the stern. "Now for my salmon head," Ma says. Whenever she fishes, she throws a whole salmon head out the bow for a monster halibut.

The bait bomb line slackens and I reel in the busted bag. I grab a weight and put half a mackerel on my hook and drop a line for halibut, and set the rod in the holder. Usually Ma and I would be talking more, but today is serious business. Usually, you don't even need to catch a fish when there's a calm day with sun streaming through the breaking fog—it's enough just to be out on the water. A banner day, as Ma says. And Mutts and Uncle Dude and Uncle TooSoon missed it.

Ma is lying on top of the cabin, stripped down to a T-shirt, covering her face with one of Mutts's old baseball caps. I'm on the deck, back propped against the cabin, half asleep with the slow, easy rocking of the boat.

"Pups," she yells.

I scramble and stand up to see and something is nibbling her line.

"Come on," she says to the fish she's imagining on the end. "Take it."

There's another jerk on the line.

"Come on," she says with a raised fist. "One more." She leans in toward the holder and readies her hands to take the rod out. "Just one more."

But nothing happens. The line isn't dead, but it isn't taken either.

She shakes her head. "I still have bait," she says. "Don't you fuck with me."

And then there's a slam on the line. Ma grabs the rod out of the holder. "Did you see that hit, Pups? Look at this. You better get ready."

I grab the big gaff and put the .410 shotgun within reach in case I need to shoot this fish in the head.

"I got you," Ma's shouting. "Yes I do."

She could have a skate or shark or a record-breaking halibut as wide as an ice floe that could carry me and her and Mutts and Uncle Dude and Uncle TooSoon and Eddie and Mr. Dean off into the gulf, or it could be an old barn door someone threw in the ocean. Or she could lose this fish before we see what is on the end of the hook. It could be nothing. Junk. A snag. It could be everything. But I know that no matter what Ma reels in, it will mean what she needs it to mean, for her and for me.

THEY FIND

THE DROWNED

✦

HUMPIES
Oncorhynchus gorbuscha

A river loses strength, loses water. Scientists catch the humpies and put them into tanks and drive to the Kenai River. The humpies are released near the mouth when the reds are running. The humpies don't know where to go—they don't know the Kenai and they don't follow the reds. They don't recognize the currents of the river, or the smells, or the way the light refracts into the water and bounces off the bottom. The reds run up while the dead humpies float down. They die because they have the wrong memories.

OUTHOUSE

A woman with long, dark hair falls asleep with throbbing shoulders from fishing all day. She sits up and rummages in the cabinets for aspirin. She can't find the bottle and she doesn't want to wake the others. But her daughter wakes up and tugs her shirt.

The woman takes the girl's hand and they tiptoe out the cabin door. The girl forgets and the door slams shut.

They wince and wait for the others to stir, but no one does. They walk the short trail to the outhouse and the girl goes first, the mother standing outside. She hears a rustle and a low, throated moan. And then nothing.

The woman looks around. The girl takes a long time so the mother raps her knuckle on the door. "Shouldn't take this long."

The rustle comes closer. She sees a large, dark creature in the woods. And then nothing.

She knocks hard on the door. "Are you in there? Answer me." Did her daughter think this was a game? She stops knocking to listen. "I said answer me."

The rustle creeps closer. "Open this door." The woman kicks the door in with her unlaced boot. The wood splinters from the force.

"Stop," says the girl from inside. She opens the door. Her eyes marvel at her mother.

An animal bursts out of the bushes and the woman shoves the girl behind her. A grizzly charges toward them, running as if he's going to knock them over. The woman holds her ground. Then he stops. Sniffs the air. Walks toward the river. The bear wades into the Kenai, crossing water to reach the mainland. When they see him climb the bank on the other side, they hurry back to the cabin.

The woman remembers the first aid kit has packets of aspirin and swallows two tablets. She puts the girl back to bed. "Don't do that again."

The girl, thinking of the broken door, is soon asleep.

LOON
Gavia immer

A loon drifts down the current. The bird has a daggered beak and with his black, black head, red eyes, and white-striped wings, he's easy to spot. The loon dives down and disappears and the scientist times him, scanning for the breach. After a minute and eleven seconds, the loon reappears upstream, shakes the water off his head. There are loons and there are ducks. Ducks are never alone.

STORM

The woman's husband knocks on the door. They were looking for him. He has blood soaked down the front of his shirt. They hadn't heard a gun. Maybe the axe, but there isn't a wound. A thick, familiar smell calms them.

He stumbles over the doorway and falls. Two of his buddies carry him to the boat and he's vomiting red into the river. The woman watches the boat leave her and the island and the blood behind. "This is the last time," she says. She nods as she's nodded before, lays towels over the mess and wipes the blood with the toe of her boot. Then she dips the towels into the river, wrings them out.

The woman sits on a stump near the bank. In the stillwater, the smolt move like a storm of comets. The terns swoop down with their pitchfork tails and scoop up small fish. Seagulls on the gravel bar bicker over scraps.

THE SCIENTISTS

The scientists sit in a boat and dip tubes into the river.

"Turquoise," says one, noting the color of the water.

"Green," says another.

"Glacier blood."

"Crushed sky."

"Kenai Blue."

They test levels of sediment from the ice fields.

LIFE JACKET

The neighbors across the river have a big family. Grandma has a whip of a cast, a fluid flick of line into the water. Grandpa wears his white underwear to swim—his barrel of belly hanging out. The grandchildren scream and splash about in their life jackets. There are five boys and their shouts echo and amplify through the spruce, scaring away the moose and the mosquitoes, if mosquitoes could be scared away. The boys swim out past the dock and let the current carry their floating heads downriver. They stay in the shallow, where they can put their feet down and climb the bank. But if their feet miss, they can grab the net rope fixed to an orange buoy. Sometimes they swim farther across and spend an afternoon on the gravel bar with the gulls.

SPRUCE BARK BEETLE
Dendroctonus rufipennis

The scientists call it the plague—the outbreak of spruce bark beetles that has infested the forests of the Kenai Peninsula for over ten years. A couple of warm summers and the beetles became a blight. They have eaten through two million acres of white, lutz, black, and sitka spruce.

They are the length of a small bullet and they thrive in dryness and heat. The scientists hope for a summer of rain to contain them. The beetles burrow through the bark and chew a path to the cambium layer, the only part of the tree that is alive. They tunnel a gallery inside the host tree and lay eggs. The scientists set pheromone traps and watch as the forest turns into firewood, the dead outnumbering the green.

ROLL

The woman hunches over the reel and her long hair falls forward. Her hip's bruised blue from fishing, but she's got to anchor down with the rod. Boats move out and make a clear path as they drift down.

"Everyone wants to be you with this big ol' fish," says her husband.

They pass the end of the drift and he takes a side channel to avoid the backtrollers.

"Let's get this one in," he says.

She reels in slow and steady. The spinner flashes and he strikes with the net. The king thrashes. He slips to one knee, loses the handle. The king rolls, fifty pounds of fish wrestles out of the net. He steps in and grabs the handle, then grasps at the mesh. She reels but the hook springs loose.

"A hen," she says. "Could've used those eggs."

"Don't jaw me," he says. He throws down the empty net. "I know."

MOOSE
Alces alces gigas

The scientist has a favorite—he calls her Al and every once in a while he'll sit on the river near Bing's Landing and look for her. She has twins now and crosses to the island at night when the river is quiet. He found her on the side of the road after she'd been hit by a truck on Sterling Highway. The driver died and he didn't think she was going to pull through. The scientist visited her when she was bandaged and bruised—he'd talk to her. "Listen," he'd say. "You're the first thing I've been good to in a long time."

YELLOW PATCHES

He and his buddies cut the trees that were turning brown from the blight, where bark beetles eat and weaken the tree from the inside. The diseased trees are yellow patches in a quilt of green. They are also dangerous. The woman is afraid the closer trees might fall over and crash into their cabin. But they're laughing and she calls them a bunch of idiots with axes.

One by one, the trees crack and fall away from the cabin. They splash into the Kenai and the current pushes them toward the bank. But one won't fall. His axe wedges into the diagonal cut. The tree teeters toward cabin and land, not water. Women and kids scatter. After the boom, the cabin stands untouched. They are unharmed. He raises a bottle of beer to his good fortune.

RAINBOW TROUT
Oncorhynchus mykiss

Rainbows are the shimmering litmus, the indicator fish. If anything goes wrong in the Kenai, the rainbows tell the scientists. If there is pollution, they die. If the temperature changes too much, they die. If a feeder stream stops feeding, they die. Kiss a rainbow, the scientists say, and you'll know all the river's secrets.

A SIXTY-POUNDER

Across the river, Mom and Dad and Grandma and Grandpa play rummy and drink beer from an ice chest. They don't see the boy slide out of his life jacket on a dare. There's struggling and a shout. Dad dives in and emerges empty-fisted. Grandpa, in his white underwear, jumps into the boat and Grandma follows. They drive to the sinking boy and Grandma holds out the king net to him. When the boy doesn't grab, she scoops him with the net. He's a sixty-pounder and Grandpa has to help heave the net aboard. Grandma pinches the boy's nose— her nails making moon indents in his skin. She forces air into his icy mouth and presses his chest. The boy chokes on air and Grandma turns his head to the side. She brushes her tears away. "You little shit," she says. She pats his back. The boy spits the river.

EAGLE
Haliaeetus leucocephalus

The eagle is perched up in the tree, singing. His call jumps octaves, runs with scales. The scientist records the eagle's sounds and writes down the time of day. A boat drifts down Superhole and stops near the scientist.

"Isn't that something?" says the fisherman. He and the woman both wait for an answer.

The scientist holds up his recorder and points. "Shhhh."

"Well, if you knew anything, you'd know they sing all the time." The fisherman's boat starts downriver. "They sing opera."

THE WALTZ

Her husband has sprawled in her absence. She lies on her elbow and hip in the narrow space and unbraids her long, dark hair. The bed is high—there are storage cabinets built underneath. Blankets and waders are stashed in the gap between her side of the mattress and the wall. He rolls closer and gains inches of mattress.

"Move over," she says. "I don't have any room."

He moves, but he rolls toward her and knocks her off the bed.

The gap is narrow enough to be a problem. "Help me up," she says.

She pats around in the shadows and feels fur. And a snout. Teeth.

She screams and scrambles to dislodge herself. He grabs her legs, pulls her up. She finds footing on the mattress and runs out of the room and then outside. The whole cabin wakes with the commotion. Her husband stands on the deck with a bear head. "I was saving it for the teeth and claws." He unfolds the skin. "Harmless," he says and puts the bear head over his shoulder and fanfares off the porch. Then he waltzes, hand to paw, around the campfire. Man and bear nod in rhythm, in step.

HALF LIFE
Oncorhynchus nerka

The red swims a slow, stilted speed as if worming through sand. He swims outside the current, keeping to the edges with the smolt. His tail is white with rotting and layers of skin hang in silken scarves. A bite? Raked by the claw of a bear? The fish should be dead. The scientist steps closer and wades into the water, aiming with the net. The fish darts away.

BEETLEKILL

"We survived the oil spill and now this," says the scientist. There's division—no one agrees on how to separate the living from the dead. The canopy has thinned by seventy percent and everything under it is changing—a beetle gnaws through the bark of a tree and the salmon count drops and then a fisherman drinks himself into a ditch.

LOGGING

The boys swim strapped inside the life jackets. The jackets float up near their ears. The river brings a tree to them and they swim to the uprooted trunk lodged near the gravel bar—the amputated branches silky with moss. Three boys straddle the tree as if they were riding a horse. The other boys grab the broken-off branches and shove and push. The river catches the tree and the boys shove more. "Go," they say. "Go." The three riders wave their arms when the current takes the tree. Grandma and Grandpa clap. Mom and Dad grab the camera and start the boat. The boys are waving for the picture as they ride downriver. The fisherman starts his boat, drives fast and waits below Mom and Dad. Naptowne Rapids waits behind him.

"One snag," he yells. "And the tree will roll."

HEN

Oncorhynchus tshawytscha

The scientist hovers over the dead hen, a female king, with tweezers. He pinches a scale from the head, the side, and the tail, measures the length and girth.

"Ain't she pretty?" says the fisherman.

The scientist holds one scale up to the light—the sheer skin of a pearl. Kneeling, the fisherman leans over the scientist's shoulders, puzzled about the lengthy examination. "It's a fish."

"Yes," says the scientist.

CRUTCH

He breaks things—doors, glass, plates. He breaks bones, but only his own, and punches the walls of the cabin. Most of the time he comes home wobbly and soft and puts his arm around her and she crutches him to the couch, hoping he doesn't wake their daughter. "I love my girls," he says. "I love my girls."

BODIES

The scientists come across a body while doing research. They need to count salmon and a human disrupts the day. A human can last six minutes to six hours in the water depending on the temperature. They find the drowned don't have liquid in their lungs—they gasp in the cold water until their tracheas collapse.

CPR

The woman and her husband walk a trail along the edge of the Kenai. The husband watches her long, dark hair swoosh across her back as he follows behind with two poles and a tackle box. She stomps ahead not thinking about where they are going. He follows because he has always chased after her. This is what they do. He has not touched her hair in two months. She has not wanted him to touch her in two months. They have no children, not yet. They have a cabin and two trucks and a long-standing argument about who should drive which truck. The woman trips over a root and there is a little blood on her knee.

"Are you OK?" he asks.

"I'm fine," she says and keeps walking. Her jade ring feels tight on her finger.

The man's hand begins to sweat around the handle of the tackle box. "Pick a spot so we can fish," he says. He wishes that her hair wasn't beautiful, with tinges of red, in the sun.

She walks a minute to make a point, and then stops. "Here."

A low-throated call makes them look upriver. A moose calf is struggling against the current. His head sinks and then pops up, then sinks again.

"He's drowning," she says.

"No he isn't," he says.

The calf gains footing for a brief moment and then falls.

"He's being swept away." She starts to walk up the trail.

"Where are you going?" he asks.

She runs. She wades out into the river. He's still holding the poles and the tackle box. The calf isn't struggling anymore. He's floating. "Please," she says. "Bring him this way." She goes in up to her waist. She grabs the calf by the neck and finds the riverbed with her feet. "Help me," she says to her husband.

They both haul the calf to the shore.

She puts her face near the moose's nose. "He's not breathing."

"He's dead then."

The woman covers the moose's nostrils with her hand. She puts her lips on the moose's mouth and blows air. "Where's his heart? Where do moose put their hearts?"

"I don't know," he says. "The chest seems right."

The woman compresses the chest and tries more air. "Go get help," she says.

The man runs up the trail. If only she were willing him to live, pressing her mouth to his. Her hair falling over his face. He finds another fisherman and the fisherman tells someone to call the rangers and Fish and Game.

The calf's mouth feels like a stubbled cheek. She cups the jaw and focuses the air stream. One. Two. She crosses her hands over the chest. The ears twitch. She pumps and hears a gurgle and water spills out. She tilts his head to allow the water to drain.

When the man returns to his wife, there is a crowd. The calf's side heaves with signs of life.

His wife looks up at him and says, "I think he might be breathing."

Fish and Game comes with oxygen. "You saved the calf's life," they say.

"*We* saved the calf's life." She looks directly at her husband. Then someone hands her a bottle of water and she swishes out her mouth.

The man and woman gather their gear. They walk the trail as before. But when they're away from everyone else she turns to face him. He's holding the poles and the tackle box so he stands there and she wraps one arm around his neck and puts her mouth on his. She kisses him and he kisses her and she puts one hand on his chest where his pulse quickens under her palm. This is what they do.

DEGREES OF NORTH

Here, the scientists know north is eighteen degrees on a compass. Not zero. They don't wander into the woods without a map. Or directions. Walking from camp, following the trail of moose—they don't lose their way. Losing, as they say, is not scientific.

WHAT YOU
CAN ENDURE

In my deep swimming dreams, my mother tells me I can't come home. Not for the things I have done, but for the things I haven't. There's a story she tells about my grandfather, Fox, leaving her at a hunting stand miles away from the homestead, alone, in the dark, when she was eight. No lantern or light in late September. "Colleen, you're the oldest," he says. "Find your way." She has a rifle. Behind every tree, another tree, another shadow, or a bear. The woods so thick. No stars to follow.

"If anyone tells you to cut your hair," she says, "it means they destroy beautiful things." Her father cut her hair. For years. Hacked above the shoulders with the bluntness of practicality. His jagged cuts marked his return from Korea, from working on the slope in Prudhoe Bay. She never wore her hair short when she had a choice. She let it grow down her back, black and straight or in a braid.

She makes me feel the top point of her skull where there is a dent the size of a poker chip. "You have it too. Your brother doesn't. I have this mark and you have this mark and we were once whales." When I dream about my mother, I dream of whales.

She says she didn't love me when I was born, it took time. She needed to know I would live, survive, prove to her I was strong enough. I was four years old before she knew. She had fallen asleep on the couch after putting me down for a nap. I crawled out of the bed and found her only tube of red lipstick and painted my naked body, a toddling flame, and rolled across her white rabbit fur rug, over and over again, rolled across the walls, her bed sheets. "A little warrior," she says. "A goddamn mess of a comet."

"God is more of a whale than a man," she says. Here, the blood washes up on the shore and melts the ice. My bare feet are tinged and lapped with red. The cold snow. The blood warm and pooling from the whale's belly. They have stripped the skin and a layer of fat with chain saws. A whale out of the ocean is a mountain, a horizon, a different bend of sky.

"Did you wash your hair?" she says. "It's as slick as cod-liver oil." Which is the worst thing. A spoonful she had to choke down either before or after a dinner of rabbit stew or moose chili. Once, she found a bottle of her father's cod-liver capsules hidden in a cabinet. Fox's secret stash for himself. "He didn't want to down a spoonful of the godawful-tasting stuff. But he made us kids do it."
     "I washed my hair," I say.
     "I don't believe you," she says. But she braids it anyway. Her braids are never straight or neat—they are frayed and wild and I don't dare undo them.

We are crossing Chinitna Bay on a fishing boat. The cousins and I huddle in the cabin and wait for the Coast Guard to pass. We have too many people on the boat. Then there is shouting, "Come up, come up." A whale. We scramble to the deck. A humpback shoots out of the water, twisting in the air, white fins raised to the sky, gray back slamming into the water. My uncles are hollering and spilling their beer on the crowd of us. Another whale breaches, leaps up from under the boat, belly an arm's length from the rail. We all shrink back, me holding on to the hood of my mother's jacket. But she has a hand out, reaching and then brushing the white belly of the falling whale, the splash soaking her. My uncles net the floating bottles they threw overboard in their celebration. "Touch your eye," she tells me. "That's what it feels like."

There is a story about how I was almost never to be. My mother goes fishing for reds with her brothers who are brand new commercials in Cook Inlet. Everyone is lined out along the rift, where the water is discolored, boats stacked three hundred yards apart, each with nine hundred yards of net out for the catch. They're in an aluminum boat and the drunk captain next to them, Sarge, is driving an old wooden rig. All the crews are cobbing with the six foot rollers and then the winds change. The boats turn and all the nets tangle together and they're tangled up with Sarge. They tie up to him so they can separate the nets and Sarge is still drinking so he's no help. And they can't find a good enough tie-up and their aluminum boat keeps banging into Sarge's old wooden rig. Then the tie breaks and tears a cleat off of Sarge's port and he says to hell with it and throws his boat into drive and sucks his own net and lead line into his prop and stalls out in the middle of the ocean. The seas roughen up with bigger and bigger swells, until they're twenty feet high and their boat is slamming down into the troughs and they've finally tied Sarge's dead-as-bricks rig to theirs. Ben sends my mother to the front to hang the big orange buoys off the side for bumpers. On the way back, she's holding on to the rail with her left hand in front of Ben who's driving in the cabin and sees his face scare as the boat pitches wild and the deck drops out from underneath her. She hangs on to the rail and dangles in the water and the next wave pitches and suddenly she's back on the deck of the boat, like she never left and Ben has that "you can't be alive" look on his face. She's soaked through but she helps untangle the mess and they crank in the net, full of fish and pallets and other drift because they have to move out of the storm. After a few hours, they anchor up and pick the nets. Over seven hundred reds with their guts falling out of their mouths, squeezed from the pressure of being rolled up. Her brothers can't handle the sight and the long, lobbing rolls of the water and take turns puking over the side of the boat and she taunts them while she eats a moose liver sandwich. "This whole day," she says, "is what we call a clusterfuck." It's one of her favorite words.

I am the sinking kind. She holds me up so I float, one hand under my neck, another under my back and I'm weightless and gliding, the water tickling my ears, my hair swirling. She swims laps around Goose Lake and I wait for her, chest deep in the water, feet padding the marshy bottom. On the shore, I see them first on my legs. Ugly and black and bloated. Leeches. And I scream. She looks down at me, calm, and says, "What would you do if I wasn't here?" People are staring and a man rushes over to help and she waves him away. She says she will do the first one and shows me. "Take the nail of your thumb and slide it under this end." I don't want to touch the leeches. I want my father. I kick her as hard as I can. She picks me up and drags me back to the truck, a hand over my mouth. On the drive, I bury my face in my towel and wail. "Hey," she says. "Look at me." But I don't. She turns on the radio. I am going to run away, I decide. I hate her and I'm going to run away and if I do and I die then she'll be sorry. She turns off the radio. "One of the leeches just fell off. When they're full, they let go."

Here, the eye of a whale is small for what a whale is. A whale is small for what the world is. I cut out the eye of the whale and hold it in my hand. There is an ocean inside of it, deep and black and storming.

"You know," my father says, "she's bluffing half the time."

"Half the time, I can't tell," I say.

Her way of saying hello sounds like "yellow." I don't know where this is from, but my uncles and aunts say it too. I think of Arctic poppies, their bright papery bowls sprouting from thin stems and rooted in gravel beds, the rock of mountains, the tundra. She makes a trip to Denali every summer to see them, little suns scattered in an endless stretch of green. "They are the same color as alpenglow," she says.

I am twelve and mad at her for dragging me along. "No, they're not," I say, and this is the last time she takes me with her.

The first time in an airplane, my mother is white-knuckled after take-off. She points at the blue in the window. "Ocean," she says.

"That's the sky," I say.

"No, we're sitting in the belly of a whale," she says. "We're waiting to be born."

"How?" I say.

"I'll tell you."

When I was young, she says I was a burrower, a little vole. And still I have this habit of closeness, even though she moves away. And once, while my father is on a hunting trip, I curl up in her bed and she turns to me and says, "I can't breathe. Why are you always so close to me?" I think now, she meant this as an honest question but what I heard was, "Get the hell away from me," and I ran to my own room. Six brothers and sisters and married at seventeen, I don't think she's ever had her own bedroom or bed.

"It's all an act," my father says. "This tough-as-nails bullshit she does." I knew this and I know this and I forget this and then I remember it again. I never undid the crooked braids she wove into my hair.

Or complained about her less-than-gentle ways with a brush. For a few minutes, untangling my freshly washed hair, she was nearest to how I wanted her to be.

"I'm glad I lived through a lot of shit so you'd have stories to tell," she says. "Because what the hell are you going to tell your own kids?" How I survived you, I think. But she'd say I was being dramatic, that when she was growing up, she was so poor she couldn't be dramatic.

"I'm not going to have kids," I say.

"It is terrifying," she says. "Maybe the most terrifying thing."

Here, the ocean is the sky and the sky is the ocean and my paddle cuts through the eyes of stars. I kayak at night, around an island without coves or inlets. I am dragging her in a kayak behind me and she is dragging a whale that moans a long, droning song.

"Talk at you later," she says, instead of goodbye. The "at" catches me every time. Not *to* or *with* and her words are a cloud of split shot coming for me. Thick as mosquitoes in July at the evening hilt of sun. My mother says she was bitten so many times growing up that she became immune and they eventually stopped bothering her. That and she smokes cigars when she's fishing to keep them away. She doesn't believe me when I say they still sting like wasps. But then a bite above my eyebrow changes her mind—my eye swells shut and my forehead puffs out. She laughs every time she looks at me while we drag for reds in the Kenai. A few months later she tells me she was a little worried. Any more swelling and she would have taken me to the hospital.

"California has made you soft," she says when I visit. And I always think, Alaska has made you cruel. But I never say it. We chop wood for the campfire and her pile is always twice as big as mine, the logs split clean. But what she doesn't know is that I lag in my upswing, I pretend to tire out because she has so much satisfaction in whistling at my uncles and pointing at her pile and saying, "Would you look at that?"

I remember being old enough to be embarrassed and ashamed and throwing my pajamas and my bedding into the tub. I turn on the hot water and pour a half a bottle of shampoo over my mess. It is the middle of the night and she knocks on the locked bathroom door. I tell her I will be done soon. "Open the door," she says. "Do you know what time it is? You don't have school for another four hours. Open the door right now." I do. She looks at the tub and looks at me and smiles. "Piss yourself an ocean," she says. "Who cares? You'll grow out of it someday."

It's everywhere on the news, in the papers. Humpback whales near California, off course and confused on their migration to Alaska. They are swimming the Sacramento River, a mother and her calf, and are ninety miles inland. The biologists play whale songs on underwater speakers to try and herd them back to the ocean. The problem seems to be all the bridges—they don't like to pass underneath them. My mother cuts out the article and sends it to me with a note that says: Whales lost in a shitty river in California and I thought of you.

When my parents visit me, I take them to Avila Beach. I teach her to body surf. She doesn't let the waves take her, struggles against their pull. What she does instead is wait for a wave to crest and then dives underneath the break and pops back up in the calm. She laughs. "Take that, you bastards." She floats on her back and rides the rolling tide. I surf a wave and my bathing suit top breaks, the metal clasp in the back. I ask her to hold it and we will walk to our towels. "I can fix this," my mother says. "Wait here." She goes back to our spot, her bag, and brings back a spool of fishing line. She is never without it. There are so many things she has fixed this way—shoes without laces, bucket handles, life jackets, loose baby teeth that needed a pull. She threads line through the two sewn loops and binds them together and bites off the end. "Fifty-pound test line," she says. "This sure ain't going anywhere."

Near the tide pools, my father points to a sea slug that has washed ashore, a purple slab of slick flesh that looks like a discarded liver. "That is the biggest damn leech I have ever seen," my mother says and winks at me.

"It's not a leech," I say, before I can stop myself. This is as close to an apology as she will ever give me.

Here, the bones of the whale are the tall skeleton of a ghost ship after the flesh is cut away. The bones are dry and smooth and the spine settles into the snow. They reach upward, ribs curving out of the ground and closing over me. I lie down and align my body, my small spine against the spine of the whale.

Her canned smoked salmon wins blue ribbons at the fair every year. She won't give her secrets away, not even to her brothers and sisters. And I am sworn never to tell them. She keeps the smoking shed my father built for her locked. She taught me the trick with rock salt, the timing, how to cut the strips of salmon, how to hang the strips in the smoke shed because "I'm not going to be around forever," she says. "You need to make yourself useful."

My first September in California, she sends me a box of mason jars filled with her famous smoked salmon. She might as well have sent me rubies. I ration them throughout the year, eat out of the jar with my fingers, the oil running down my chin. I send her the empty jars and oranges and tangerines and cherries from Bakersfield. Then my father calls and tells me not to send oranges, please, she hates oranges. There's a story about her pissing the bed growing up and not being allowed to eat dinner and starving and finding the K rations and rotten oranges her father hid in a crawl space. I send her cherries and nectarines and plums the next time and vow never to forget something like that again.

"Why can't she remember this one thing?" my father yells. She never flushes toilets. She was raised with outhouses. "I know," he says. "I'll build an outhouse in the backyard, just for her, if this keeps up." He shakes his head. "She'd kill me. But I'd be making my point."

"Do you really want to do that?" I say.

"It would be funny," he says.

"She wouldn't think so."

"We would," he says. "And sometimes all we can do is laugh and know she's not going to change."

The midnight sun sinks behind me, slips below the horizon. Before me, the alpenglow caps the mountains in a gold sheen. There is no straight line between the two—the light behind me and the light I see ahead. The downing sun reflects off the horizon, the sky and air and clouds and ice, and appears as a faint mirror of itself on the opposite side. There is no straight line between my mother and me. Between us is a homestead and a hunting stand and acres of thick woods and she is running and I am running after her.

"She never finishes her story about being left out in the woods on the hunting stand," my father says. "Have you noticed?" I have always finished the story for her. I assume she makes it back, she finds her way. "Ben told me. She was lost," he says. "And had given up and thought a bear might be tracking her. She shot into the air. Her mother wrestled a rifle from her father and answered with gunshots to guide her back to the homestead."

My mother tells a story about the first sailors who reach Alaska. They have never seen whales before. Two humpbacks breach near their boat, heave their bodies toward the sky. The sailors scramble for their guns and shoot at the water and wait for them to reappear. The humpbacks breach again and their strange white markings are a target for bullets. And how could the sailors have known? The whales mean no harm. They have no teeth. They are only coming up for air.

THE LAST GREAT
ALASKAN LUMBERJACK SHOW

HOT SAW

You check the choke on the chainsaw. Pull the starter cord. The engine is warm, but sputters. You pull again and the engine floods. Turn the choke and throttle off. Pump the cord several times. Move the choke. Pull the cord three times. You wait, pull again. There's a buzz. Then everything dies. You fall away from each other.

"We could try other things," you say.

"It's no use," Hyde says. He doesn't know you've made him a doctor's appointment for next week.

"I'm going crazy," you say. You've been noticing how everything else in the world is tall and erect—your bed post, trees, utility poles.

"How do you think I feel?" he says. He escapes to the bathroom. The pipes whine as he starts the shower.

All you want to do, lately, is "Yes. Oh god, yes." And you don't care how—you'd have sex with Hyde's knee if you had to. Or his elbow. Now he's in the shower, and he'll have that clean smell, and of course there's the basil oil you sneak into his shampoo, and you won't be able to take it. He says he's stressed at work, a new lineman is being a pain in the ass, the son of one of his good friends. He says he needs a little time, and that was a month ago. In the meantime, you're having sex dreams about the letter *L*, once with the letter *L* and the letter *Q*, but usually only the *L*. *L* is cold, quick, efficient. And you wonder if this is normal, these fantasies with members of the alphabet. You tell

Hyde most of your dreams, but not these, no, not these. Should you be worried? You can't even think of a man you know whose name starts with *L*. No Lukes. No Lyles. No Linuses. Or maybe it stands for every single loser you've ever dated. If you two weren't having this problem, he'd probably think your dream was hilarious, hang a huge cardboard *L* on the bedroom ceiling as a joke, find ways in public to say, "Gracie just loves *elk* meat."

Last year you dreamt that sperm had become airborne, like a virus, tiny particles in the air impregnating anyone who breathed them in. So Moody was going to have a baby, and Slug had gotten a girl pregnant. Hyde woke you up, said you were talking loud in your sleep again. You told him. He laughed, howled really. You said, "Who the hell needs to think about this kind of shit?" Then later that summer, at your cabin near the Kenai, the cottonwoods were blooming and he said, "Oh my god, honey, run for your life, airborne sperm." He pointed to a flurry of tufted seeds sailing in the air and picked you up and ran. You thought, "This is why I fucking love this man."

AXE THROW

Your daughter Moody has perfect aim. She says, "I hate you. You're old and ugly so you think I have to look like shit too." The axe flips blade over handle, over and over, and lands in the center of the painted bull's-eye on your chest, rib bones splintering like wood. You could slap her heavily made-up face. That's not your style. You could walk out of her room and never speak to her again. But you say, "You're right, honey. I'm ugly as all hell." And then you laugh. The inappropriate laugh—once the word "coma" put you in a rapturous fit even though it was in reference to your estranged father, his stroke, and he never woke up. You want to take her face in your hands, and press so hard, fast-forward ten years, make her a creature that doesn't terrify you. But you would rather she be terrifying, sharp-tongued, a fighter. You know that as long as she's fighting you, she's hearing some of what you're saying.

"Let's slam all the doors in the whole damn house," you say. "Better yet, let's light this place on fire. Let's start with all the crap in your room." You pick up a pile of the slutty clothes she borrowed from a friend and throw them on the bed. No daughter of yours is going to risk hypothermia in order to be ogled by junior high boys. "Get me a match," you say.

"It's not crap," she says. She doesn't believe you'll do it.

"Go," you say.

She brings back a box of matches.

You strike one up.

"You've totally lost it," she says.

"I haven't lost anything," you say. You blow out the flame. "Not yet."

When you were eleven, your mother took you salmon fishing at the usual spot on the Russian River, just the two of you. You were covered in fish slime and scales because your job was to bonk the salmon after they'd been ripped out of the river. She said, "I want you to know that soon you're going to think you're right about everything and I'm wrong about everything. You're going to say terrible things to me and you'll actually mean them." You told her you would never do that. "You will," she said. "You'll even wish I was dead. And I want you to know it won't stay that way. I want you to remember me telling you that this would happen." And you did. You'd start to heat up with rage over curfew, and suddenly turn cold, just to prove her wrong. Your mother, the bomb defuser. It worked on you, but not on your brother. And not on your own kids.

LOG ROLLING

You have to keep talking so you don't lose her. You're both balancing on a log in the river and at any moment, she could slip, fall back into the churning water where you can't reach her.

Your mother waits for the long-term care nurse to go clean the bathroom. She makes a cat claw with her arthritic hand and hisses. "I don't like her," she whispers.

"You don't like anybody," you say.

"That's true," she says, with satisfaction.

"The kids are good," you say, to keep things moving. "Slug just got his license. So now he drives Moody to school in The Beast. They're growing up so fast—makes me want to lock them away in their rooms."

"They locked me away in this room," she says. "They did."

She stares into your eyes, studying, questioning. She once made you promise never to put her in a home. The log rolls faster and you pedal.

"I brought you blueberry pie," you say. "Would you like some?"

"Let's go out for pie," she says. "I can leave, you know." She teeters over the edge, arms flapping.

"Let's eat here."

"You sound like my husband," she says. "Have you met my husband?" She crashes into the river. The wake makes you wobble.

"I've met him," you say.

"Where is my fat son?" she says. "Have you met him?"

Your brother has never been fat, unless you count infancy. He is all muscle, and sometimes you think even his brain is a bicep. He does not come to visit your mother. You feed her small bites of pie with a spoon. She worked on the recipe for years—lemon zest and fresh basil bring out the blue in blueberry.

"We could go out for dinner," she says. "Just push my chair."

"Not today." You're alone, the log slowing under your feet.

You kiss her goodbye and she grimaces. Her white hair is pulled back into one long braid. They were going to cut it and you begged them not to, paid them extra for the braiding. She wouldn't care if they gave her a buzz cut, but you would. You're the only one who visits her. At home, the rest of the blueberry pie waits on the counter. You scoop out the middle with your bare hands.

UNDERHAND CHOP

You stand on the log with the axe raised over your head. You have to aim true so you don't hit your own feet. "What is it?" you say. "What the hell is the matter?"

"Life." He shrugs.

You'd have never let his nickname Slugger be shortened to Slug if you knew it was going to be prophetic. Same with Moody, called as such because neither she nor Slug could say Melody. Some days, you wonder if you should ever have moved to the city six years ago, if you could call Anchorage a city. Hyde's commute would have been too far. But you miss the river. You change tactics, and turn around and chop the other side.

"We're going to the cabin," you say. "You and Moody are skipping school tomorrow. This is a fucking family emergency." And what you mean is, you need these kids to shape up, or take shape, emerge out of their oily skin suits and be human again.

"I'm not going," he says.

"You're going," you say. "Or you find another place to live. I'll send you to Uncle Jack."

"What?" he says. "You can't do that."

"Yes," you say. "Yes, I can. Start packing. Tell Moody."

The Beast is a 1975 Suburban that Hyde has rebuilt and had forever, and will have forever, unless the thing blows up into a million pieces and even then, you think he'd try to repair it. The Beast is known to have problems starting up at times, which might have something to do with the spark plug you are removing to make sure Moody and Slug don't take off in the middle of the night to avoid going to the cabin. You hide the spark plug in Hyde's toolbox in the garage.

Moody rushes toward you when you walk through the door. "I have to go to school tomorrow," she says. "You can't do this. It's against the law or something."

You stand on a new, fresh log, and raise the axe. "When have you, Miss C Average, ever wanted to go to school?"

"Ever since Dallas or Dakota or whatever his name is," says Slug from upstairs.

"Shut up," says Moody.

"You know the rules," you say. "No dating anyone named after a city or a state."

"Oh my god," she says. "You're so ... you're ..."

You pull the blade out and swing again. "Maybe if you got better grades you could think of something," you say.

"You're ruining my life," she says.

"Sweetheart, you ruined mine a long time ago," you say, with a final chop. "Go pack some clothes. Grab some work gloves while you're at it."

JACK AND JILL BUCK

Hyde comes home from his twelve-hour shift at two in the morning. He immediately showers. You sit on the closed toilet seat and tell him about Moody and Slug, taking them to the cabin. The basil oil in his shampoo is steaming all around you.

He pokes his head around the curtain. "Get your ass in here," he says. His eyes are smiling. "Show me what Moody thinks is old."

You throw off your pajamas and step into the tub.

"I had to fire Ander's kid," he says, soaping his chest. "Told him to go redo his safety certification and we'd talk about giving him another chance. Thought he was going to get himself electrocuted today." He spins and rinses.

"How did Ander take it?"

"Huge weight off my shoulders." He leans and backs you up against the tile, breathes into your ear. "Which means..."

This is what should happen next: You each have a grip on the saw. The emcee says 1–2–3–Go and it's a synchronized give and take, the teeth cutting through the white pine log. No kinks or bends. No snags. Sawdust flying because this is your event.

"Dammit," says Hyde.

You wait.

"I guess it's time to see the doctor," he says.

"Ten a.m. Thursday," you say.

He turns away. You put a hand on his back. "This is what's happening," he says, and he gets out of the shower.

You said the same thing when you found out you were pregnant with Slug and Hyde made you an appointment to see an AA sponsor.

SINGLE BUCK

Jack has set up camp in a small cabin near the Kenai River, down three gravel roads, then a dirt path just wide enough to fit a truck. He and Jean separated. He told you it was a mutual decision. She told you it was a mutual disaster.

She said, "He puts the S.O.B. in sober, you know what I mean?"

He said, "She puts the bitch in bitch."

Jack is outside with a small chainsaw when you arrive. Log pine cuts, three feet tall, are lined up on a picnic table. He's working on one cut with small slashes. You didn't know he'd taken up chainsaw carving. The cast-off carvings sit on the ground. A wing with a missing tip. A split beak. Some are hacked in half. A deformed bunch of almost-eagles stare at you, a flock of fuck-yous. Jack's blue T-shirt has a bib of sweat and sawdust.

"Gracie," he says. "Was wondering when you'd come find me."

"Thought I'd see if you wanted to go fishing."

"You're checking up on me," he says.

You pick up a broken wooden wing covered in prickled cuts that are an attempt at feathers.

"Besides, I'm always fishing," he says. "That's my problem."

"I got two problems back at our cabin," you say. "I put them to work chopping wood."

"The good ol' lumberjack cure," he says.

"They just don't know how good they have it," you say. "You know how it is."

"I once threatened to make the kids eat earthquake stew. Jean threw a fit."

"How they taking the news?"

"They're not surprised."

You hold up the eagle wing. "I want one of these once you get it right."

"Can't fucking drink," he says. "Have to do something."

"Then let me take you out on the boat."

He shakes his head. "You drive like shit. And I know how you like to go alone."

TREE CLIMB

You pick up the boat and trailer from the lot behind Bing Brown's grocery and liquor. You've heard people say every woman needs her own room. What every woman really needs is her own boat, her own river. At Double R Marine, you sell boats to fishermen and hunters and guides, and rarely to women. You see the disappointment in the bearded faces when you're assigned to help them, instead of Reed. They think you don't know what you're talking about, and you dig in with your spikes and it's a race to the top of the tree. Question after question. A test. Sometimes you make up stories and tell them your father was a guide on the Kvijack. Or the Talkeetna. If they double-check your answers with Reed, he says, "She does rivers. I do ocean. We've never had a problem." And then they believe that they need a jon boat with a detuned fifty. You memorize river regulations every year and Reed says you're a damn dictionary.

You drive the boat to the launch. Someday you'd like to have a cabin right on the river, tie the boat off on your own bank where you can slay reds when they run. But for now, it's enough to drive to Superhole and take the inside drift around the wide curve, hug a gravel bar and drag the pocket for rainbows. Forget about selling boats. Forget Moody and Slug and Hyde. Forget Jack who won't talk about your mother or visit her. Forget your mother who is forgetting you. Here, you are hook and line.

SPRINGBOARD CHOP

"There's more wood to chop," you say to Moody and Slug. You know they didn't chop as much as they could while you were fishing. They're not happy with you. "Get it all out there," you say. Anger and hormones and being powerless and young. This is the exercise they need, or the exorcism. Build a bridge, you want to say. Build something. Stop scowling and hunching. Build a monument worthy of your misery. Carve a giant hand flipping off the sky. Just do something.

"For how long?" they want to know.

You want them to double their stacks.

"Then what?"

"Pizza at Magpye's," you say.

Hyde shows up. A day early. "Switched some shifts around," he says when you walk toward him.

He nods at Moody and Slug and their axes. "How'd you work that?"

You put your arm around him. "Look at what we made. You and me, buster. What were we thinking?"

"I was thinking I wanted more of you in the world," he says. "More of us."

"We're idiots," you say.

"Well, someday it will be just us idiots at the cabin, fucking our brains out."

"Promise?"

If they ever ask you what it's like. Being a parent, an adult. You know what to say. That's if they live that long, if you don't kill them first with too much wood chopping. If they don't kill themselves or ride in a car driven by a drunk friend named Skully or Beevo. So many ifs and you can only shoot so many of them out of the air.

If they ask, this is what you will tell them: The river is rising too fast. A flash flood. You chop a slot into a tree, chip into the trunk with four swings. You insert a plank into the slot and climb onto it. If the river soaks the plank and your feet, you make a higher mark with the axe at waist level. Put another plank in the slot and climb. There's no telling the number of people you fit on this skinny piece of wood. Too many. And not enough. But this is how you stand on water.

RESOURCES

Campbell, Robert. *In Darkest Alaska*. Philadephia: University of Pennslyvania Press, 2007.

Holsten, E. H., R. W. Thier, A. S. Munson, and K. E. Gibson. *The Spruce Bark Beetle*. Forest Insect & Disease Leaflet 127. U.S. Department of Agriculture Forest Service, 1999. http://na.fs.fed.us/spfo/pubs/fidls/sprucebeetle/ sprucebeetle.htm.

Juday, Glenn P. "Spruce Beetles, Budworms, and Climate Warming." *Global Glimpses* (Center for Global Change & Arctic System Research newsletter) 6, no. 1 (April 1998). http://www.cgc.uaf.edu/newsletter/gg6__1/beetles.html.

Pacific Salmon. Wildlife Species Information. U.S. Fish and Wildlife Service. http://www.fws.gov/species/species__accounts/ bio__salm.html.

Ridolfi, K. and K. Wehrly. *Oncorhynchus mykiss*. Animal Diversity Web: University of Michigan Museum of Zoology, 2006. http:// animaldiversity.ummz.umich.edu/site/accounts/information/ Oncorhynchus__mykiss.html.

Roth, Bill. Photo of the snow sculpture *Qasida*. "Fur Rondy Snow Sculptures." *Anchorage Daily News*, March 1, 2010. http://www. adn.com/2010/03/01/1162990/fur-rondy-snow-sculptures. html. I read a description of the photo at http://www.adn .com/2010/03/01/1163165/rendezvous-snow-sculptures-tickle .html.

"Whales in the Delta." *Sacramento Bee*, May 29, 2007. http://www
.sacbee.com/static/newsroom/maps/whales/.

The title of "Mr. Fur Face Needs a Girlfriend" was inspired by the Mr.
Fur Face Competition held at Fur Rondy in Anchorage.

The title of "The Last Great Alaskan Lumberjack Show" was inspired
by The Great Alaskan Lumberjack Show in Ketchikan.

THE FLANNERY O'CONNOR AWARD

FOR SHORT FICTION

CPSIA information can be obtained at www.ICGtesting.com
Printed in the USA
BVOW032236221012

303685BV00002B/2/P